Praise

The Small Backs of Children

"Thrilling storytelling with universal appeal . . . gripping."

—*Entertainment Weekly*

"Gorgeous, scary . . . a breathtaking rush to read . . . a provocation on the power and dangers of art . . . Yuknavitch has written a sensational book."

—*Library Journal* (starred review)

"I have never felt so wrung out by a novel and yet simultaneously invigorated . . . a terrifically good novel and powerfully written . . . draws to great effect on the fraught overlap between women's bodies and minds. . . . [I]t's refreshing to be punched in the gut by a book now and then."

—*The Paris Review*

"Wild . . . Yuknavitch's sex scenes are remarkable among current American novelists, not just for their explicitness but for the way she uses them to pursue questions of agency, selfhood, and the ethical implications of making art. . . . Not since Kathy Acker . . . has an American novelist written so vitally from within this tradition, claiming the body, especially the female body, as her primary subject, and writing polymorphous sexuality not only so explicitly but with such joy."

—*The New Yorker*

"Explosive . . . fascinating and nuanced . . . fierce in its vision, with captivating prose that carries its own momentum. . . . Yuknavitch has created a reading experience that is uncomfortable and dazzling, with a vital intensity that grabs at the gutstrings."

—*Los Angeles Times*

"This erotic, beautifully disturbing exploration of sex and violence is a fast, lyrical read, but don't let the brevity fool you—its effects will linger long after the last page."

—NPR

"Yuknavitch's formal and linguistic playfulness . . . places her in the vanguard of contemporary American writing. . . . [The novel's] liberatory experimentation with voice . . . places it squarely in the realm of the most accomplished experimental fiction . . . a tour de force of multi-voicedness . . . masterful. . . . Yuknavitch's writing in *The Small Backs of Children* is ever lovely and precise. Its bold imagery and fragmentary style recall *The Lover*, by Marguerite Duras, even as its meditations on photography and war, not to mention Yuknavitch's aphoristic style, can't help but invoke Susan Sontag. . . . [A]n important book . . . difficult in the truest and best sense of the word."

—*Los Angeles Review of Books*

"A novel for the bold of heart . . . [t]he violence is fierce and proud . . . the story begins with one of the most arresting scenes I've ever read. . . . Yuknavitch . . . writes with great beauty and daring."

—*New York Journal of Books*

"[F]urious and tender . . . an intensely corporal, potently feminist, tenaciously written work as alert to animal resilience as to the capacity for bruised and battered suffering, for desire, for ecstasy . . . may slightly rip your heart out . . . . *The Small Backs of Children* is a very different work than Siri Hustvedt's ferocious, feminist art-world novel *The Blazing World*, but the two are kin, and it's easy to imagine Hustvedt's hulking rebel, Harriet Burden, taking a liking to this defiant girl, who is daring, inquisitive, and pliable enough for survival."

—*Boston Globe*

"[I]ncendiary . . . Patricia Highsmith by way of Kathy Acker in a highbrow thriller . . . Yuknavitch is a gifted writer. . . . The women of *Children* buck and kick and break down the doors—and expectations—erected by the endless parade of 'someone else.' . . . A radical, necessary step . . . [Yuknavitch] tells the stories that need to be told, not the ones that are easy to hear."

—*Kirkus Reviews*

"In this daring novel, Yuknavitch takes a provocative look at the intimate relationship among love, art, and sex in a group of emotionally scarred artists who want to save one of their own. . . . Yuknavitch's novel is disturbing and challenging, but undoubtedly leaves its mark."

—*Publishers Weekly*

"Yuknavitch is rewriting our cultural mythos here, carving a path for women to be fiercely creative and alive with desire."

—*Minneapolis Star Tribune*

"Yuknavitch uses language like a spade, sharp, delicate, digging us deeper into meaning and empathy for a child's bodily experience of horror. I read some pages ten times."

—*Sydney Morning Herald* (Australia)

"[W]ill wreck you and leave you feeling grateful. . . . The novel is hot, erotic, damaged, informed, and redemptive. . . . Yuknavitch's precise, sensual language knits you tightly to the imagery. . . . [A] wakeup slap."

—*Bitch* magazine

"As brutal as it is beautiful, Lidia Yuknavitch's powerful novel *The Small Backs of Children* is a meditation on how we survive and heal despite the violence we may encounter."

—*BuzzFeed Books*

"[A] fierce and passionate writer." —*The Millions*

"Gorgeous . . . a love letter to the power and pulse of art . . . deeply complex and layered . . . exquisite in its lyricism and its ability to articulate and amplify the experiences of suffering and survival . . . powerful and necessary. . . . [I]f you're a writer, you'll wonder how Yuknavitch did it."
—*The Nervous Breakdown*

"A challenging tour de force that sounds gruesome (war, sexual abuse, violence against children) but is really a standard-bearer for choice, whether in how we love, who we save, or what we write. In Yuknavitch's nimble hands, the corporeal and the fictional intertwine. . . . Yuknavitch writes about art, violence, sex, ferocity, willpower, and womanhood with explosive force, in a language that evokes modern mythology. . . . There's an urgency to her exuberant language; one wants to devour it. . . . Yuknavitch is in such command of her language that she can, without fear, let it lead her into places most contemporary writing does not go. She is a writer of great power, prepared to grapple simultaneously with the lofty verities of art and the dark needs of the body, battling her way to a ceasefire with humanity." —Literary Hub

"Packs in action and intrigue aplenty, but it's no straightforward thriller . . . a stunning novel . . . beautifully examines the fractures of loss and the myriad ways we can recover from it . . . a wild ride."
—*Huffington Post*

"Brilliant . . . a brave act of family making . . . an examination of the spectrum of creation—whether of self or art—and how often creation can uneasily exist along with destruction." —*Electric Literature*

"This violent, gripping thriller about loss will rivet you and stretch your mind in new ways." —*Bookish*

"If you want a novel that's going to swallow you alive this summer, turn to Lidia Yuknavitch, whose *The Small Backs of Children* is the kind of book that goes straight for your heart and your mind. Fearlessly, Yuknavitch takes you to war-torn Eastern Europe to ponder ideas of love, loss, and identity you'll keep thinking about well after the brief novel is done. This one's important . . . Yuknavitch's writing is a sizzle wire. Her fierce prose will jumpstart your heart and electrify your brain . . . a provocative and thrilling jolt of a book. . . . [Yuknavitch] is a writing warrior." —*Bustle*

"There are writers and then there are *writers*. The kinds of authors who form sentences that seem to come from deep within the body, an element of themselves. Yuknavitch is that kind of writer; one who puts the blood, the water, the self on the page. . . . [A]ttempting to sum up the plot doesn't express just how good this book is. Read it for the sentences. Read it to understand how and why art is made."

—*Men's Journal*

"[Yuknavitch is] writing toward a great purpose, toward a revolution. . . . Yuknavitch approaches her characters' humanity in a way that veers left before traditional storytelling and makes its own road. . . . Yuknavitch uses language in a way that is so sensual it is almost sexual . . . the love child of Kathy Acker, Jean Rhys, and Carole Maso . . . fierce . . . subversive . . . unique. . . . Yuknavitch has succeeded in fulfilling E. L. Doctorow's charge: 'The reason we need writers is because we need witnesses.' *The Small Backs of Children* proves once again that Yuknavitch is witness to the kind of stories we ought to read." —*The Rumpus*

"[B]old . . . a compelling, moving, at times emotionally exhausting read, one that gets under the reader's skin in dozens of ways."

—*Vol. 1 Brooklyn*

"Terrifyingly prescient . . . [an] incendiary blast of a novel."

—*Public Books*

"Astounding . . . visceral . . . [Yuknavitch] creates images that reverberate. . . . [T]he novel's lyricism and cultural insight soar . . . a deeply moving piece of public thinking . . . intensely felt, beautiful."

—*Lambda Literary Review*

"[D]ense and fine . . . a magical package . . . intensely erotic and savage . . . epic. . . . The power of the pen is mighty here." —Fictionaut

"This book made me feel emotions I didn't know I had."

—LitReactor

"Yuknavitch's first novel for a big publisher is a big winner . . . raw and devastatingly direct . . . fearless and skillful . . . brings to mind the writings of Virginia Woolf . . . a powerful and lyrical novelist . . . bold. . . . With *The Small Backs of Children* Lidia Yuknavitch propels herself forward as a complex writer, a novelist who eschews traditional storytelling, an original author who has much to tell us in her distinct and very personal voice." —*Oregonian*

"The uncompromising Lidia Yuknavitch reinvents the novel . . . she's one of a handful of writers currently shaking up literature at its very foundations. . . . Risky . . . raw . . . [*The Small Backs of Children*] really comes at you." —*Portland Mercury*

"[Yuknavitch is] very much a writer that we need right now. . . . Anyone who really loves storytelling? This is the book for them."
—*Word of Mouth* (New Hampshire Public Radio)

"[C]all[s] to mind the late work of Virginia Woolf and Clarice Lispector's short stories while also slyly rewriting Vladimir Nabokov's 'Lolita.' . . . [Yuknavitch] liberat[es] the novel from the prepackaged box in which it's often sealed and delivered." —*Milwaukee Journal Sentinel*

"By balancing visceral scenes with meditative moments, Yuknavitch creates a remarkably layered novel that seems to expand and contract as you read it." —*Orlando Weekly*

"[F]ierce, cyclonic . . . offers a punch in the face to the idea of art's irrelevance . . . a wild and beautiful novel. . . . Yuknavitch . . . has a point of view and a fragmented and fractured visionary elegance in her poetic, allusive punk-infused voice. She grabs readers by the throats and immerses them in an intense, wrenching fictive world, but lets them up for air through careful structuring and pacing. . . . There's an electric main vein running down the center of this book and if you hold on, you'll feel charged and buzzing—and alive. Because that's really it—this is a novel about being alive and what it takes to stay alive . . . a brave, bardic book." —*Buffalo News*

"Promises to be her biggest hit yet . . . intense, provocative, and full of interesting feminist implications." —*7x7* magazine

"Masterful . . . promises to stay on the skin long after the reader has turned the last page. . . . Tightly wound, pacy and provocative, *The Small Backs of Children* is destined for greatness."
—*The Irish Independent*

"Packs a powerful punch . . . everyone is going to be talking about this book." —*Boat International Magazine*

"Fierce and explosive . . . a gripping and intense narrative ride that will haunt you for days." —*Lit Up* (podcast)

"Yuknavitch has the rare and almost magical ability to write beautifully about things that are horrific . . . a gorgeous, heartbreaking tale of friendship, guilt, redemption, and healing." —Powell's

"There are a handful of books that have changed the way I move through the world. *The Small Backs of Children* is one of them. It follows me now, like a friendly specter, whispering in my ear about truth and art and beauty. Lidia Yuknavitch writes with sly, subversive, nervy, compassionate madness. She is one of the great American writers."

—Chelsea Cain, *New York Times* bestselling author of *One Kick* and *Kill You Twice*

"You can make the case that Lidia Yuknavitch is the most compelling writer alive. Devastating and thrilling, this book folds and curls into a gorgeous tapestry of obsession [and] dares you to look away. I felt bewitched, possessed, destroyed, and yet I'd do it again."

—Porochista Khakpour, author of *The Last Illusion* and *Sons and Other Flammable Objects*

"A great novel by a fiercely original writer . . . intelligent yet accessible, provocative in the best ways, complex yet tightly plotted and riveting. The characters are beautifully drawn, and together their story raises important questions—about violence, art, sex, and survival—that are both timely and enduring. And the writing—the writing is sublime."

—Whitney Otto, *New York Times* bestselling author of *Eight Girls Taking Pictures* and *How to Make an American Quilt*

"All my youth I gloried in the wild, exulting, rollercoaster prose style and questing narratives of writers like Henry Miller, Charles Bukowski, and Jack Kerouac, but cringed at the misogyny; couldn't we have the former without the latter? It turns out we can, because: Lidia Yuknavitch."

—Rebecca Solnit, author of *Men Explain Things to Me*

"One of the best books I've ever read. Simply astonishing."

—Rene Denfield, author of *The Enchanted*

"Lidia Yuknavitch isn't afraid of anything. . . . Or maybe she is afraid, and keeps wading into the deepest water anyhow. Either way, we need her sudden cyclonic no-holds-barred wisdom more than ever."

—Pam Houston, bestselling author of *Contents May Have Shifted* and *Cowboys Are My Weakness*

"Unsettling as a fairytale . . . reads like a meta-detective novel seeking to solve the most vulnerable of human mysteries: How can I still be here when you are not? As she follows a young Eastern European girl whose family is killed by a bomb blast—and a host of characters who mount a plot to rescue her—Yuknavitch moves through narratives and structures like a literary banshee seeking a body. Fast, visceral . . . a gunshot meditation on art and violence . . . I couldn't put it down."

—Vanessa Veselka, author of *Zazen*

ALSO BY LIDIA YUKNAVITCH

o o o o

Dora: A Headcase

The Chronology of Water

Her Other Mouths

Liberty's Excess

Real to Reel

The SMALL BACKS *of* CHILDREN

◦ ◦ ◦ ◦

A Novel

LIDIA YUKNAVITCH

HARPER PERENNIAL

NEW YORK • LONDON • TORONTO • SYDNEY • NEW DELHI • AUCKLAND

HARPER PERENNIAL

P.S.™ is a trademark of HarperCollins Publishers.

HarperCollins books may be purchased for educational, business, or sales promotional use. For information, please e-mail the Special Markets Department at SPsales@harpercollins.com.

FIRST HARPER PERENNIAL EDITION PUBLISHED 2016.

Designed by Leah Carlson-Stanisic

Library of Congress Cataloging-in-Publication Data has been applied for.

ISBN 978-0-06-238325-9

20 OV/LSC 10 9 8 7 6 5 4 3

This book is for Andy and Miles Mingo,
who brought me back to life.

I go where I love and where I am loved,
into the snow.

—H.D.

Disambiguation

Muse : /myooz/noun : Origin /Greek

- In Greek and Roman mythology, each of nine goddesses, the daughters of Zeus and Mnemosyne (the goddess of memory), who preside over the arts and sciences. The Muses were both the embodiments and sponsors of performed metrical speech: mousike (hence the English term "Music") was just "one of the arts of the Muses." Others included Science, Geography, Mathematics, Philosophy, and especially Art, Drama. Inspiration, stimulus.

- A woman, or powerful force personified as a woman, who is the source of inspiration and agency for a creative artist. An imagined feminine.

Part One

The Girl

You must picture your image of Eastern Europe. In your mind's eye. Whatever that image is. However it came to you. Winter. That white . . .

One winter night when she is no longer a child, the girl walks outside, her shoes against snow, her arms cradling a self, her back to a house not her own but some other. It is a year after the blast that has atomized her entire family in front of her eyes. She is six. It is a house she has lived in with a widow woman who took her in—orphan of war, girl of nothingness.

But that night has never left her . . . it is an unrelenting bruise. Its blue-black image pearling in and out of memory forever. Nor will it ever leave her body, the blast forever injuring her spine, a sliver of metal piercing her flesh and entering her, so that all her life she will carry the trace of that moment between her vertebrae.

And then again her mind moves to the moment of the blast,

the singular fire lighting up the face of her father, her mother, first white, then yellow, then orange and blue, then black, then nothing, her head swiveled by the force of the blow away from them. This does not frighten her. What used to be nightmares have transformed into color and light, composition and story. It is with her now. Lifelong companion. Still life of a dead family.

The snow begs her senses now, and she wishes she had a coat. She wishes she had tied her shoes properly, worn proper socks. The moon, however, makes an entire setting for her motion, and in this way she feels . . . lit up.

She hears something not her and not the night and not the white expanse waiting before her. Her feet are cold and she can suddenly feel how numb her hands are, shoved in her armpits. She does not know, at first, what she is hearing. At first it seems like the sound of hummingbirds' wings, but that is not possible. A fluttering whir, quiet as secrets, there and then gone.

She remembers her father: his eyes, his word.

She hears it again, then, and knows it—a wolf caught in a trap. She looks down near the fence line. It is a wolf, beyond beautiful, with its leg caught in a trap. She moves closer, aware now of how the cold is biting into her. She studies the wolf. The wolf is smart. It is almost finished. She thinks, in only the briefest of thoughts, of releasing it.

The wolf is nearly free.

In its freedom it will lose a leg.

It will be worth it.

She holds perfectly still.

More still than a dead person.

Which she has seen, many times—a corpse in snow.

She watches the wolf chew its own leg by the light of the moon, by the rhythm of its journey. The moon makes its slow arc in the sky, and inside the moon's movement, reflected in the girl's eyes, the wolf finally frees itself.

It is then that she does something pure bodied. Child minded. She goes to where the rust-orange and black metal of the trap sits holding its severed limb, to where blood and animal labor have reddened and dirtied the pristine white of the snow—like the violence against a canvas. There, without thinking, she pulls down her pants, her underwear, squats with primal force, and pisses and pisses where the crime happened. A steam cloud moves upward from the snow and the blood as the relief of rising heat warms her skin.

Her eyes close.

Her mouth fills with spit.

This is how the sexuality of a girl is formed—an image at a time—against white; taboo, thoughtless, corporeal.

She opens her eyes.

The piss smell and the blood smell and the youth smell of her skin mingle. She licks her lips.

The wolf runs.

It runs three legged, like all damaged creatures, across the snow.

She thinks: this is true.

She thinks: this is a life.

She thinks: I do not want to die, but my life will always be like this—wounded and animal, lurching against white. She bends down and rubs her hands in the blood. She lifts her hands, her eyes, her heart to the heavens, in the space where they say god is, a god she has never known, a god she will replace with something else. Her small hands make what might look to an outsider like a prayer shape. But she is not praying.

She closes her eyes. This is the night it happens. She looks down at her red hands. She laughs, up. She bends down and wrenches the severed limb from the trap. And then she runs toward a self.

What is a girl but this? This obscene and beautiful *making* against the expanse of white. This brilliant imagination, inventing meaning.

The Writer

A woman must have money and a room of her own if she is to write fiction.

What a crock. Virginia, fuck you, old girl, old dead girl.

I am in a midnight blue room. A writing room. A room of my own making—with its rituals and sanctuary. I can see my husband and son in the next room fiddling with a video camera. Looking at them together makes my heart feel crushed like a wad of paper. I reach down below my desk and pull up a bottle of scotch. My scotch. Balvenie. Thirty year. I pour myself a shot. I drink. Warm lips, throat. I close my eyes. I am not Virginia Woolf. Do you know how many women can't afford the room, or have no help, or scratch away at things in bars, buses, closets? I much prefer a different line of yours, anyway: Arrange whatever pieces come your way. Or this: Someone has to die in order that the rest of us should value life more.

I know something about death.

Inside everything I have ever written, there is a girl. Sometimes she is dead, and haunts the story like a ghost. Sometimes she is an orphan of war. Sometimes she is just wandering. Maybe the girl is a metaphor, or maybe she is me, or maybe a character who keeps coming.

I write her and write her.

Sometimes I think I am following her into another place or self. She is leading me. Directing the traffic of my life.

I've always been suspicious of narrators. And of characters, for that matter. Of the figures of speech we create to stand in for people. Or selves. There is something weird and unnatural about them—how they do what we tell them, how they obey. I don't trust them. Narrators especially. Chickenshits.

I have been someone else many times.

I was a competitive swimmer for eighteen years.

I was a secretary in a lawyer's office for a year and a half.

I was a waitress for eight days.

I was a heroin addict for six years. China White.

I was married two times—eleven years, first, and now going on thirteen.

I have slept with women for twenty years.

I have slept with men all my life—from the time I can first remember things—if by sleeping with men one means sexual encounters with men and their dicks.

My father figures here.

My mother's suicide attempts happened when I was eight, eighteen, and twenty-eight. Before she got it right.

I flunked out of college once, quit twice, then battled my way through to the telos of a Ph.D. Became a teacher of literary things. Whatever those things are.

I have been drinking scotch for twenty-six years. Balvenie, thirty year.

Off and on.

I was incarcerated the first time as a minor for eighteen months.

I was incarcerated the second time, of age, for eight months.

I was incarcerated the third time for eight nights.

I was a mother the first time for nine months, just nine, then the mother of a dead daughter. Now I am the mother of a son. Strange and alive boy.

I was depressed at age eight for one year, but it just felt like being underwater, which was familiar to me, the swimmer. I was depressed the second time at age eleven for two years, then again at eighteen for one more. Then I went under—depression—second self—and resurfaced violently. Recurringly.

Everyone I love is an artist. None of us knows what we mean. Oh, we pretend that we do. Some of us win prizes and lift strangely off the surface of things; others of us toil away, making our own labor into an overrighteous romance. Some of us have jobs, or tenure, or family; some of us are rich, others ride the grant trains; some of us are homeless or nomads, others addicts or recovering or lapsing. Aren't we all just shooting for a life where art matters?

What a cast we make.

My brother the New York playwright, winner of American status, seizer of material wealth.

My now-husband the filmmaker, driven to create images for audiences who long for escape from that other movie, life.

My onetime lover the war photojournalist, image purist, traumatized by her own shooting star.

My friend the performance artist, generational do-over, her youth our only chance at passing something on. Fake legacy.

My dearest and fiercest friend, the poet, lover of women and sexual excess and language.

My ex-husband the painter, who held in one hand a brush he used to create new worlds, and held in the other the gun he tried to shoot me with.

We make art, but in relation to what exactly? All the artists we admired from the past came out of the mouths of wars and crises. Life and Death. We come out of high capitalism. Consumerist monsterhood. Even when our lives went to shit, they were still just our lives. Our puny, overdramatic, American lives. And where we are from—our so-called country, defined by the smell of a well-made latte, the silent hum of an all-consuming war machine, and the televised face of Oprah—are we *for* something? *Against* something?

All our artistic origins have been atomized. Dead fathers and brave mothers against the kitsch and speed of this glossy and disposable new century.

I love them all. I write them all. Does love make art?

What is the story of a self? What is chronology? The history of a life? Which story should I tell to make a narrator, an American woman writer at forty-five—which plot, which pathos? Because any writer's life knots are embedded in whatever story they tell.

I have invented hundreds of selves. Men and women.

I have peopled the entire corpus of my experience with fictions.

Who is to say they are not I? I them?

And if I tell the truth, this once, will it be any different from all the other tellings? How? In what sense would it matter?

We are who we imagine we are.

Every self is a novel in progress.

Every novel a lie that hides the self.

This, reader, is a mother-daughter story.

The Violence of Children

When violence comes to the door of a child's house it is not comprehensible to her. Even if she has some small awareness of the war or violence or danger surrounding them, the truth is that the faces and hands of the people in her family, the horses in the barn, the mouse she is secretly keeping as a pet, the potatoes frozen underground, the kick ball made from animal skin and straw and twine, the glass in the windows and the shivering walls of the house are infinitely more real to her. She cannot help it. The sound of a mother's voice singing her to sleep, the alto of a father reading a poem, the smell of a brother's skin just before dreams, the moon's giant eye, all of these overshadow whatever violence is at the door. Think of Anne Frank writing about trees.

When violence came to the village near the girl's family's house, there was no stopping it coming to her door, her body, as well. The six-year-old body of a girl.

Seventeen times against the wall or in the barn: *You move or scream or say anything I will kill them all. In front of you. First I will torture them and then I will kill them.* Her eyes as dead as she can make them. Her arms as limp as she can make them. Her heart as hidden as she can make it. A soldier's cock entering the thin white flesh of a girl, into the small red cave of her, the fist of her heart pounding out be-dead, be-dead, be-dead.

Counting.

In the world around them, violences became perpetual. Men were sent to icehouse prisons. Women and children were raped repeatedly. Children were bought and sold on the open market. Systemized violence became part of ordinary experience, so that it was not unusual to see—not blood and body parts, but displaced fear and horror in micromotions. The tremor of a hand or the twitch of an eye; bullet marks in the side of a house; women with scars around their eyes and mouths as deep as archeological finds; little boys who could not sit in chairs.

There were blood and body parts too.

And the end to reality every other day.

America—that great maker of realities—blind and deaf to all of it.

A story that never existed, since no one ever saw it represented.

And then, one day, her family was blown to bits.

An inconsequential blast.

Just an anonymous explosion.

Behind the girl, a photojournalist on a prestigious assignment. In that moment the girl's mouth opened wide as a child's scream, but no scream emerged, either in the instant of the blast or forever after. Her breath caught in her lungs like an animal's. Her eyes locked, her skin blanched, bloodless, her hands and arms flying upward, without control.

There were people around on that day to whom she could have run. There were, of course, soldiers; surely even amid their brutality there was one kind heart, one man who could still remember his family and would at least send her to an orphanage. There were other people nearby, neighbors from the village, watching or hiding. And, without her seeing them, there were foreigners: underground photojournalists chasing the perfect image, reporters dying to lasso the story, "human rights" workers milling about in "safe houses."

But she did not run toward any people. None of the people there had anything to do with her. When the blast happened, she ran to the woods. In her smallness and her quickness she disappeared, a girl's body torn from the heart of love.

What luck for the photographer. To be so accidentally present. And what cocksure instincts, her editor would say. Right on the money. You can see how she got the assignment.

We think of children as innocent and helpless, she scribbled on a note to her editor, but really this is and isn't true. Think of how many children survive the darkest atrocities and violences. Hundreds of thousands of children. Armies of them. Not news. She folded the note in two and sealed it in with the undeveloped film before handing it over to the press shipper.

••••

In the moment of the blast, the girl could have died with her family.

But she did not.

And so, now, she runs.

In her running, her mind leaves her.

And she can hear nothing but her heart, the blast making her deaf.

There is a great white silent empty in her running.

She runs.

She runs to the dark oncoming line of the forest.

Her hands making little man fists of anger.

The edge of the forest coming into focus.

Her teeth clenching in her mouth.

The moon, Ménuo, big white eye in the dark.

It is snowing.

Miraculously, the snow will cover her tracks.

The branches of trees opening their arms.

Her panting.

Finally the forest holds her.

She keeps running.

The forest is black and white—illuminated through the trees by the moon.

She runs until her legs and lungs cry *child*.

She stops.

She looks up at the night sky, visible through the treetops.

She looks at her own breath making fog in front of her face.

Then she walks and walks, placing her hands on the bark of trees for courage.

Tree by tree, her breathing comes back to her.

She has no thoughts, just this body.

The forest is made of tunnels. Each tunnel opens into a deeper place in the woods, and the deeper she goes, the more surefooted she feels. Many times she has been hunting in these woods, and even as her mind is filled with cotton and electricity she knows she is far from alone. There are, for one thing, trees. And animals. Deer, rabbits, hawks, wolves. Ménuo, the moon. And Saulé, on the other side of the night, the sun mother, goddess of all misfortunates, especially orphans. And Aušrine, the morning star, and Vakeriné, the evening star.

And of course the rebel camps.

So when her legs have nothing left, and her skin is as cold as a dead person's, it is fortuitous that she is knocked to the ground by a boy made into a man by war. She thuds thankfully in a small heap to the forest floor. He puts the long hard of his rifle against her throat, which she cannot feel. He shines a flashlight in her face. He smells of boy and rifle and dirt and sweat. She cannot see him and is glad. She makes her body limp, she makes her eyes dead, and then she loses consciousness, smiling.

When she wakes, she is inside a small makeshift tent. She is on the dirt of a floor, covered with blankets. Her feet and hands and cheeks feel very hot and they sting. A woman wearing the clothing of a man is petting her head, saying *ssshhh.* Almost like a mother. *Drink this.* She sees a submachine gun hanging from the woman's shoulder, rocking slightly, accompanying the woman's voice. In the corner of the tent, a man is being dressed in women's clothing, his gun and knife at his gut being wrapped with scarves. Then she sleeps again.

The next morning the sun is there and the woman is gone, and there is the same manboy with a rifle standing over her. She can smell it's true. He gives her a nudge in the ribs with his foot. Get up, he says. She gets up and finds that she is wearing heavy boys' clothes. He hands her a pair of boots that have straw and leaves stuffed into them. Then he tells her that he and another man will take her to the edge of the forest. Do not cry, he says. You are lucky to be alive. Luckier still not to be in a Gulag, little pig. I said we should put you in a hole in the ground to watch for the enemy—you could squeal if you saw anything. If you cannot fight, you are nothing. I said we should use you as bait. He spits on the ground. Then he takes his dick out and pisses right near her feet. The steam rises between them. I said we should kill you. I don't care if you live or die.

She is not scared. She can hear him and she concentrates so hard on his face and mouth she can feel her eyes become bullets. She wants the boots. Violently. She wants the coat—stained and torn and smelling of piss. He grabs his dick and moves toward her and she readies herself to go dead, but he just rubs it on her arm. Harder. Faster. The reddened muscle of a boy. She counts the dead air. Soon he comes in a hard hot spurt on the coat. She puts the coat on without hesitation, looking him in the eye. There is a scarf on the ground with some of his piss seeping into it that she would snatch up even if it were on fire. She wraps and wraps it around her head, covering everything but her eyes. She wants the pouch of dried-up bread, the canteen of dirty water, the broken knife. She wants everything he is giving to her.

They march her to the edge of the forest. They point to a spot across the whitened landscape. They say there is a farm there. From where they are, the spot looks like it could be anything. Or nothing. She begins to walk. She could be walking into a whitened oblivion. She wonders if they will shoot her after all. She thinks she hears them laughing. She turns only once to look back. He is pointing his rifle at her. She sees a wolf out of the corner of her eye, watching her, or maybe all of them, as it backs into the forest and she moves slowly forward, toward some unseen form in the distance.

The Writer

My daughter. Say it—hold it in your mouth, look at the words: *born dead.*

To be told there is no pulse at the precise threshold of birth—water breaking. To be told to deliver anyway. Death.

The day birth came at last, the labor had lasted two days. I nearly gave in. I kept thinking, To what end? It seemed true that at any point I could simply surrender to the pain of an ordinary body and . . . leave. I looked at the people around me—my eyes puffy, my skin done in—and thought, I love you, I love you all, enough, good-bye. But I did not leave, and the dead girl was born.

I expected her to be blue, and cold. Lifeless. I expected her to feel dead weighted. I expected to die, quietly and with soft breathing, from holding her.

But she was not blue, and she was not cold; she was like the weight of the history of love in my arms. Her skin was flushed and her eyelashes were very, small, long. Her lips were in the hue and shape of a rosebud. Her hair . . . she had a small halo of almost-hair. And her hands were curled in the shape of something tender and potential. I was holding life and death—those supposed opposites, those markers of narrative worth; a beginning, an ending—all at once in my arms.

I did not die.

But I could see the grief coming like a towering wave of water about to swallow the world. When grief comes, you must breathe underwater. I knew I didn't have much time. You know, hospitals will not allow you to take a dead baby home with you. You must make arrangements, with the hospital or with a coroner or a morgue. They send in "grief counselors," and, if you let them, god help you, clergymen.

I just wanted her body. I wanted her body more than I have ever wanted anything in my life. And so I did what I had to do.

I asked the poet—my lifelong rival, beloved friend, a borderline criminal—to steal her from that fucking place for me.

You will think it sounds impossible, but it was not. It was laughably simple. The poet was close friends with an attendant, an addict, at the morgue where I agreed to send her. The morgue had its own crematorium. In lieu of her lifeless body, a little pig covered in a soft blanket was sent down the metal road to the fire.

Instead, I took her to a place where a river empties into the sea. I drove there alone, with her perfect weight next to me in the passenger's seat. I talked to her and sang to her and recited poems to her. When I got there—not anywhere anyone would be—I placed her in a backpack that also contained kindling and sage and waited for night. The wind was unusually still, and the surf had the rise and fall of breathing. The moon's giant eye looked on. It was the end of an Indian summer. I removed my clothes. I held her body to mine for a long time. Until it came, the great flood. Animal sounds came from my throat. Nearly all of the night we rocked that way.

When a dead calm came over me, I made a pyre of sticks and sage and the only thing I had to give to her, my hair. All of it I could sever. Great clumps of American blond. I placed her body and my hair atop the pyre and lit it on fire. I watched her burn. I did not cry while she burned. The smell of burning skin and ocean and sage. I did not look away. I collected the ashes in the morning and walked into the sea with them. So there was a moment when we were together in the same waters.

Then I entered a cataclysmic silence, a white vast, for nearly a year.

After grief—strange sister self—left me, I thought, stupidly, that I could live my life, and love the artists who are in it, and carry on by writing. I gathered them together for meals, for art events, for films and readings and gallery exhibits. I thought I could narrate over everything. This . . . what I am still doing now. I am writing a journal of the girl. But I don't know if I can withstand it. I hear my husband and son in the kitchen, making dinner, setting plates, and I close my eyes. My heart is beating me up.

I am an American woman writer. I am in the room I write in. The room with midnight blue walls. Dark red carpet against deep brown hardwood floors. Two windows with long off-white curtains. And books . . . books everywhere—on floor-to-ceiling shelves, on the floor, on the desk, piles of literature, art, photography, philosophy. The colors of their spines and covers the colors of skin, blood, fire, water, night. A black iron lotus Buddha with a broken hand that we glued back on—me and my husband, my now-husband. A good ironic metaphor. Various feathers from birds I have come upon: eagle, heron, crow, crane, and swan. Bowls of rocks. A photo. The cat's food bowl. Desperate talismans, the colors of blood and night and the bottom of an ocean. And the scent of someone over-saging a room because they are afraid they will make something to death.

I think things like, Be brave. Hold on to voice. It's your only chance. Pick up the glass of scotch. Bring the amber liquid to your mouth. Drink. Large. Hold it there. Close your eyes. Move your goddamn hands before your mind makes a mess of it.

I see an image of a dead girl—an arrested image.

My breath jackknifes for a moment.

It's the girl. I don't know if she will kill me or save me.

Women and Children

The white is flat.

The girl does not look at her feet. She looks straight ahead, willing the shape in the distance to become the farmhouse they said it would be. The sky has smudged out the sun. Under each footstep she knows there is death: land mines and the graves of disappeared people. If she looks down it could kill her. Part of her wants to be blown to oblivion.

She is nothing but body: her legs and chest are burning, her jaw aches, her eyes swim in their little sockets. Then a farmhouse and barn emerge like ghosts before her; there is light in the window of the house. And another small forest—black-and-white-barked birch—on the other side of this place. She stops at the fence line and stares down. She sees her own breathing in white erratic gusts.

Little by little, her breathing eases. She can feel her tongue and teeth, her ears. She is at a crossroads: a child's violent will to survive lodged in her chest where her heart should be, but an utter indifference along with it. Dusk is falling. She closes her eyes. When she opens them, she ignores the house and walks to the barn and chooses an empty horse stall next to a black mare. She finds a thick horse blanket, as worn and coarse as an animal's skin. She buries herself in straw and the smell of goat, horse, pig, and chicken. When night comes, she is nothing more than an animal in a barn.

She doesn't think about entering the farmhouse. For there is a woman in the house; she catches glimpses of her in the window at night. Her mind is on the eggs she sucked down raw. On the mason jars filled with root vegetables. On the milk she squirts from the goat's teat into her mouth.

Next to the barn, she double-steps ten feet one way, then ten another, until she has walked out a square in the snow. With her broken knife she goes about clearing the snow away so that dirt and dried-up grass and thistles and weeds and rocks emerge. Then she digs. By the time the woman comes out of the house and spots her, she is all hands and concentration. She doesn't even look up.

If the woman is thinking, Who is this girl, what is she doing, it has no effect on her digging. The girl is just fingers moving, nothing more.

The woman is stricken by the loss of her husband to a Siberian prison. Everything she sees has the same weight—next to nothingness.

She sees the girl when she gathers the eggs. She sees her when she feeds the animals. When she puts the horse in the field. When she milks the goat. She sees her each day, furiously at work on the ground. She sees her pile wood from the woodshed, cover it with kerosene, and light it on fire with matches from the barn. The two of them do nothing to care about each other. They take note of each other's tasks and respectfully circle around them.

This happens for days.

The girl never comes to the door of the house; she never needs anything.

It goes like this. Six days, seven.

Then one day the woman is patching the roof and falls. The girl looks up for an instant, turning her small face to the falling. The woman's body, then head, hit the frozen ground with a great *thud*. She is momentarily stunned. Then she opens her eyes and her body comes conscious. She has hurt her back, though not irreparably. She turns her head there on the ground and looks at the girl. For a moment, their eyes lock. Then the woman heaves herself up and goes in the house.

The next day the woman does not get out of bed.

In the dirt, the girl builds a forest surrounding the village, and begins the hard work of digging a trench for a river.

The next day, when the woman feeds the animals, she also brings the girl a jar of water, one half of a cooked cabbage, and a lump of sugar. She places it in a box just inside the barn.

Each day the girl builds more and more of the small village in the mud and snow and rocks and thistles. A small mound here for the center of things. The old church, the butcher's, the small building where handmade paper was crafted, the store for ink and paint and pencils thick as a finger—pieces of charcoal in thin waferlike lengths or in rows like thumbs, oil paints she has dreamed of. She builds people with small bits of dead grass, twigs, little stones. Lining the streets. For trees, she uses pieces of the ends of trees. For walls, shale set upon its side. For the hills just outside the village, mounds of mud. Streets and bridges are made from pebbles and bark. For the sun, hay is wrapped and wrapped into a misshapen ball, set upon a hill, endlessly setting or rising. And for the photographer, the last person she saw before she shut out sight, a speckled stone.

By the time the girl's eyes had risen to the fallen woman's head on the ground, she was already lost in some other world. When their eyes met, the girl's felt nothing. She turned back to her city of dirt and her hands caked with mud and continued her work. There is but one thing left to build and that is nearly unimaginable. Her house. Her father, a shattered starscape. Her brother, blown to bits like tinder. Her mother . . . she shuts out the image.

She flashes to another image, smaller, that lives between her ear and her jaw. It is an ordinary image, routine as a baker's truck delivering bread, or a woman carrying her great bags of groceries from the market, a dog barking as she passes, a flock of birds lifting to the sky as hands in prayer. It is ordinary because that's how memory replayed over and over again works—each act of remembering deteriorating the original and creating a memorized copy. It is herds of soldiers, the colors of stone or wall, lifting up from stone or wall as drawings taking on life, coming into motion, marching; the mud-thudding of boots and heels. It is the gray-green uniforms moving in unity, erasing human as if human were a smudge on a perfect black-and-white page all the shades of pencils. It is the faces of men passing by in rows and rows, the flesh changed color and texture to some thick putty ball plopped atop shoulders, the eyes black. It is bodies bludgeoned and the splatter of red onto the gray-green arms onto the stones of the gray street onto the gray walls; it is the bodies going limp as a fish brought to shore thunked on the head and rendered lifeless and dropped into the pile of the day's catch; it is the almost-eyes from behind windows or doors not there and yet witnessing, it is the light—not night and not day, an in-between, not horror or joy, something without a name or place, something without a color. It is a mother and a father and a brother fading from color to ash, or a woman in a house mad with grief, her love lost to white, or just a child stubbornly representing a city in the snow.

Two casualties of war: childless mother and a motherless child, happening near enough to steal each other's very breath.

On the ninth day the woman takes the food straight to the girl. She squats down on the ground. The girl immediately starts to point to her creations and name them. The woman nods. They eat carrots. When the girl is finished naming, the woman points to a smooth blue-gray stone, which seems to inhabit a forest of sticks.

Vilkas, the girl says.

Wolf.

On the tenth day, the girl finishes the city and enters the widow's house.

The Photographer

Hello. It's me. I wouldn't write unless it was important.

It began with insomnia. When I lived in Ocean Beach. Remember O.B.? I was sleeping on the floor of some musician's apartment. Pitch-black, lingering smell of pot, and all the things I thought would slow down and get better if I stepped out of my photojournalist life and into this . . . beautiful fantasy of a man's life. Jesus. Look at him. He sleeps the sleep of the dead. Or of a clueless child.

I lifted the sheet up and looked at my tits and my belly and it suddenly occurred to me, This witless manboy is in trouble. I could roll over and kill him with this middle-aged body—bloated and difficult to roll, laden and slow to sink when dropped in water. Every year a woman's body degrades. Five pounds. Ten. Fifteen. Fuck.

What was I thinking when I got with him? Do you remember? That I would mother him? Me, a smarty-pants middle-aged childless overachiever? A maternal figure? Are you laughing yet? God.

I remember walking into his bathroom that night thinking, I'd go down on a dead man for some high-powered sleeping pills. And looking in the mirror. And nearly coronarying. What is it—this thing of a woman going from the drive and whir of her thirties into the thick and slow-bodied drag of her forties . . . is it just age that ages us? Or something else? I could feel the small feet of crows stomping around at the corners of my eyes. I could feel my ears growing longer, heavier, ridiculous. I could see my own nose growing for the rest of my life, changing my entire face, elongating it and drooping and dropping it as if everything about my face were becoming an enormous, bulbous fishing weight.

My head hurt. I heard a voice. The immensity of the image—larger than any systematized god or belief. Only the image, arrested, can liberate us from the lie which suggests that life tumbles forward toward some meaningful end. The arrested image is an artifact. When one stops the hegemony of life in motion, the truer fiction emerges. We are each simply an arrangement of particles of light, she said. We are none of us anything if not a glimpse of something fleeting and minuscule, weightless as air.

Photographs replace memory. Photographs replace lived experience. History.

The voice was mine.

The me that drives me to be something beyond a woman.

And I remembered who I was. And I knew I had to leave. So I grabbed my car keys and my camera bag and I walked out to my car and I left. Naked. Just like the night I left you in the desert, the only night of my life, I think, sometimes. My camera. Your body.

As I drove away between rows of ice plants on I-5, I thought, Take photos. It's all you've got.

When you try to slow down and rest inside the life of a regular American woman, you fail. And you fatten up like a hog. Just leave it. There is no other life for a woman like you. So I took the assignment. And now they're telling me I've won the prize of all prizes. Perfect.

Am sending you my notes. You're the writer—please figure out how we can "do" something with them? Will send framed photo when I can. I don't know what it means any longer.

All my love.

Notes—War Zone—Eastern Europe—Day 23

The night is cold as fuck and the color of ash and soot . . . even with all this snow. Ironic: newspaper colored. The town has already been shot to shit, and the soldiers look to me like jack-booted thugs from some B-rated movie, really, ignorant killing machines with ill-fitting uniforms and contorted loyalties. Only their boots and rifles look lethal. Every corner of every building is shot away, making the little village look like pieces of itself . . . ghost structures. There's no telling rubble from real here. None of this has made the news, it's just gone on and on for years without end, the supposed end of one war giving way to the endless micro-violences of forever. Nobody even knows where I am or what I'm doing or why. Not even me. The ground stinks of blood and shit. Domesticated animals—horses, sheep, pigs, dogs, and cats—wander around or stand like idiots in the paths and streets. There is a commotion up ahead—they want something—badly—and they are yanking people from homes like snatching tissues from a box. They want something—or someone—and they are moving as one entity of brute force against these small families. I don't know these Baltic languages in any real sense—just bits and pieces enough to stay mobile. I'm only able to be this close because I'm dressed as a garbage man, as my interpreter and guide told me to. We've been given the duty of clearing corpses from the street. It's easy to snap shots from this distance, in this grayed-out light, smoke and dirt and night's falling covering my hands and sound being swallowed up like it is, though my guide looks angry with every shot I take. He doesn't think it's worth it. A photo, he says when we are in the cave of his house—what use is that against what is happening here? Do you even know where "here" is? Do you even know what our story is? How long this fight? I know why you are here. You are here to catch the soldiers committing atrocities. But only because you are American. You want to shame them, to make a big story of their brutality. Where were you when we needed you? During your so-called Cold

War, with your promises of nuclear attack—your threat to obliterate them—we counted on you. After the war, we hid in the woods for years waiting for you. You offered us guns and money, and we accepted them. But you did not attack. And so we have been left to fight alone for all of these years.

Sometimes I think my guide wants to kill me. But he merely hands me bread and hot tea with something that helps me to sleep at night. The look he gives me is one of dismissal. I am nothing, or less than nothing, so it costs him little to help me or kill me.

We move closer and closer to the edge of this hulled-out village, its people overexposed and dead with fatigue. We pass through the rubble of some kind of town center building. We pass what was once some kind of café or bar, its windows as black as the eyes of a corpse. We pass something—a schoolhouse, maybe, its doors boarded up like a shut mouth. We are some ways behind them, and more or less part of the detritus. Soon they are at a house that is barely in the village at all. We are able to approach mostly because of our giant, horse-drawn wagon, full of rotting bodies—it seems part of the mise-en-scène.

What I see next doesn't seem possible, but the first form to emerge from the house is a girl. She looks to be about ten or so. Her hair spreads in waves of nested coils around her face, down her shoulders. Unbelievably, she walks straight toward them. She is wearing the clothes of a boy—and soon a second self, her brother, and her father and mother, come rushing out like blood after her. There is some yelling back and forth, and then it happens—a blast from I don't know where disintegrates the father, mother, and brother just at the edge of the girl's body, missing her in some terrifying accident of a fraction. They blow up right before her eyes, her hair lifting for a moment, so that she looks as if she may float skyward, her arms up and out, her face glowing so white that her eyes look like blue-steel bullets, her mouth open in the shape of an O.

I remember how the ground shook.

I remember the camera going off. Shooting before I fell.

I remember her hands—palms white—fingers spread.

The light from the explosion must have acted . . . like a flash. A perfect flash.

There is yelling and a lot of smoke. Not all the soldiers are there any longer. No one even looks at us as we hobble away, fear bringing bile into my mouth, my guide so angry he nearly fractures my arm pulling me away, and when I turn my head back to the action, I think I see a girl running toward the woods.

The girl—she disappears. She fucking fades to black, and in our rush and fear all we try is to stay alive, to make it out of that scene without more bloodshed. Back at my guide's claustrophobic home, after my body quits shivering and my heart stops fuck-whacking and my lungs act like air sacks again—I mean, JESUS, how much closer can one be to an explosion and not be inside it—instead of thinking about what I just witnessed, I am seized by a random memory. It's you. It's the photos I shot of you the one week we were lovers. A random flashback like a bulb exploding.

Your skin. The mound of your sex. How you were right when you said I'd leave, how I was mad at you, and all I could see even while I tried to kill your quiet with my tongue was the image of your face against my leaving—against the image of me, a naked woman getting into a car and flooring it at dusk, leaving a dust swirl and tracks like an open wound with no hope of suture—doing anything she can to get the fuck out of the story. The image of your mouth. My leaving.

And then I feel some kind of back of the head WHOP and you are gone, your image, and I'm in this war zone again, and a random family comes tumbling through the door. The only word for their fear is their faces. Bread and hot beef broth appear. We all sit there in the silence of our traumas and eat. So bread and broth can save your life. And memory has no syntax.

For a long time, no one says much of anything. The mother hums to her children—two boys and a very young girl. The father stands in front of the fire with the look of a father. He and my guide share cigarettes with god knows what rolled up in them. Finally I walk over and they let me share—thank fucking baby jesus there is something LARGE and hallucinogenic in the cigarettes. Things get swirly like smoke and my skin stops revolting against me.

The mother keeps looking at me like I want to eat her children but she doesn't stop me. The only one who will talk to me is the oldest boy. Most of what he says is a runaway train. I can only understand him in bits. First I try to take notes, but then I give up. What the fuck am I writing down?

I can barely understand him. His life is ten of mine. He is maybe twelve. Fuck.

What I am able to understand is this: this family is going into the woods. The father is a schoolteacher and the mother is afraid to live in her own house, having just watched her beloved neighbors disintegrate. I ask him, Won't they simply chase you into the woods? "No," he says, and he is vehement with it. I think he tells me, The rebels are in the woods. They have camps. They will not chase us there. I think he tells me, If they chase us they will be cut into pieces and fed to the wolves, and we will watch, and we will laugh and sing and dance and spit on their souls by firelight.

I begin to cry. The mother puts her hand on my arm but doesn't look at me. In this house, in this village no one in America knows the name of, in this war no one in America gives a flying fuck about, I am at home. I want to stay. Inside the danger, in front of a fire in a tiny space with people I can barely understand. This is the quick of history. This is a reason to be alive, inside the fear of being dead every second. I look at each of them one at a time. They have no love or care for me. But each of them meets my gaze. When I bring my camera out between my hands, small and without drama, they let me.

It is enough.

I don't want any part of my former life. I want whatever is inside this small mechanical box to kill whoever I ever was. These words, the only trace left of me— I give them to you.

The Photograph

The photo of the girl is nascent.

At the moment of the blast, light through the lens hit the film like a fist of electricity. Silver halides swam frantically in their chaos, unstable as history waiting for someone to point a finger and give a name to it. In the calm thereafter, the image was invisible, latent, hidden on a roll of black-and-white Kodak film inside a Mamiya camera.

She, alone among her peers, has resisted other ways of capturing images. Even when it meant bidding for film and cameras in foreign countries.

At night, in a house, in a lull between villages and violences, that roll of film—the only one she cares about—is removed from the camera, shoved quickly inside a condom, and crammed into the photographer's sports bra. There it sits all night, inside a prophylactic against flesh and moisture and dirt, against the ever-twitching chest of the photographer, who monkey-paws it now and again until sunrise.

The next day, this roll and several others are handed over to a journalist who is making for a bigger city with better phones and digital processing and fax machines and, thankfully, bars. Lots of bars. The roll of film in the condom jostles around with its siblings in an oblong athletic bag with a great white *swoosh* sewn on the side. Inside the bag it is dark and smells of chemicals, paper, sweat, and coffee. The journalist drives the Saab with one hand and scratches a scab on his driving hand with the other. The scab chips off the flesh—*success*—and a blood mouth the size of a peanut opens on his hand. He sucks it. He hopes he has the number of the woman he wants to bed tonight. He pictures it in his wallet between dollars. He tries to remember if she has a television.

When the car stops in a city, many hours later, the journalist dumps the bag of mismatched and varied media onto the desk of a foreign correspondent. With hands like Michelangelo, the correspondent organizes the media for their various journeys. His eyes ache. When he exhales there is a kind of moan. He's getting too old for this. They're giving him less and less face time and more and more makeup. His hangover sits with pickled wrath somewhere between his gut and his throat. He rubs his temples—ice picks to the brain. He stares at the roll of film. Who still processes film? What kind of prima donna is she? His hands carry the strain of his life in their tremors as he packages the film roll, lumbers onto a moped, and transports it to the last processor around.

A great white processing machine eats the film. In a space as dark as death, the film slides into its emulsions. The silver halides reduce; the first trace of the girl's image makes its shadow self. Then the film is fixed and washed and dried, all inside the belly of the machine. A worker supervises the mass production of image after image, but the day the girl's image emerges out of the mouth of the machine the worker is eating a sandwich and absentmindedly stroking himself in the back room and misses it. Thinking mostly about his semi-boner and wishing he had another sandwich or ten, he packs it up with the negatives after his break and shoves it all into a prepaid FedEx envelope.

The FedEx guy on the sending end is on speed. His eyes are darts.

The FedEx dude on the receiving end is stoned. He chuckles a little stoner laugh as he heads out in his magical white truck.

In America, the editorial assistant in charge of going through the daily photo deliveries every four hours moves a pile of black-and-white photos around on a desk, and the picture of the girl emerges. The editorial assistant pulls her hand back. The girl is farther in the foreground than she should be. It is because she has been blown forward, away from the explosion and toward the camera. She looks as if she is coming out of fire, her eyes bullets headed for the lens. Behind her, fire and smoke, and an arm and hand reaching out. At first, the editorial assistant doesn't want to touch the photo. She notices that she's holding her breath. Then she snaps out of it and carries it quickly to the editors. It feels weirdly hot in her hands. She thinks she maybe feels the warmth of blood between her legs. On the desk of the editors, the photo glows with potential. Men eye it and analyze it and judge its merits relative to other pictures. The curation happens quickly, however. There is only one image that matters.

All of this happens without the photographer. The photo, after all, is out of her hands. Later, it will be professionally and lovingly developed again—this time by hand, not machine.

Calling from a crackling phone in some hole-in-the-wall, she does give the editorial assistant one direction: Make sure the writer gets a copy of the photo. Send it right away. Write "this is the girl" on a scrap piece of paper. Then she hangs up, smiling, thinking of the writer. Hoping for her intimacy.

And so, the first time the girl comes to the house, the writer is at work on her novel.

She takes the package into her living room.

She pulls the cardboard strip that slits the belly of the package open.

Briefly she pictures the photographer's hands.

She reaches inside and pulls the framed photo out.

It is wrapped in brown paper.

Scrawled across the front of the paper in some stranger's hand: *This is the girl.*

A whisper of star-cluster emotions move briefly through her heart. She stares at the handwriting.

She unwraps the photo.

She looks.

Her pupils dilate, as they do in the dark, or when we shift focus from something far to something near, or when we are very much attracted to something, or when we enter an altered state.

Yes. This is the girl.

The Hands of a Boy

Once, when her husband was out of town at a film festival where his work was appearing, the writer took their son on a photo shoot. She bought two Kodak Instamatic cameras. She drove to the edge of the big river running through their city. It was a gray day—the kind of gray sky where the clouds look like they are holding the rain in their arms. They ran alongside the river along the river rocks, brushed their bodies inside patches of river reeds, examined a dead seagull drawn inland, collected little shells and stones. She showed him how to use the Kodak camera. His hands more adept at making things than he had language for. His cheeks two blooms.

They took photos for hours.

When she had the film developed, she took joy in his images—barely focused close-ups of rocks and sand and detritus. Odd-angled images of water and broken glass. The big gray of the sky that day. The eye of the dead seagull. And then she saw an image of herself that he'd taken. Her blond hair blowing across her face, her too-red winter wool coat, her arms so outstretched for him that they look as if they are about to pull off and away. It may be the truest image of herself she's ever seen.

She makes a promise to herself: *Remember to let go. When the time comes. Remember that you must.*

Part Two

The Widow's Watch

The widow hears the girl make noises in her sleep. One night, when she hears the girl moaning, she pulls a blanket around her own shoulders and pads her way to the girl's bed to rub her back, to take her from nightmare to otherwhere, but when she arrives at the body of the girl she realizes she is not moaning.

She is laughing.

Another night, the widow is again pulled from sleep by the sound of the girl—she is walking toward the front door. Is she sleepwalking? The widow believes it: Whatever this girl has been through, it must have lodged in her subconscious forever. Likely this girl will be haunted the rest of her life. But again, when she reaches the girl, when she extends her arm out to wake her or stop her from leaving the house, she sees that the girl is not opening the door.

She is instead placing her cheek against it. She is kissing the door. She is smiling. Then the girl curls up on the floor at the base of the door and sleeps deeper.

Then there is the night the widow hears singing. Is it singing? Again she rises from her bed and moves toward the girl's bed, but the girl is not there. The widow moves silently toward the front door, but the girl is not there either. The widow's heart makes a small tightening fist in her chest. But then she looks toward the kitchen window and there the girl stands, looking up and out, the moon lighting up her face. Eased by the sight of her, the widow listens.

The girl is not singing. In her hands is a tiny brown owl. The owl chirps and trills in small rhythms between the girl's palms.

The Photographer

The night the photographer won the prize, she called the writer. From the bar where her colleagues took her to celebrate. A very prestigious bar in the country of the war zone, in a city big enough to be untouched by the violence, at least not visibly. One of those cities of money and bars and galleries and governments and five-star hotels, all over the world, that sit next to human atrocity. Later, she would send each of their friends their own framed print of the black-and-white photo. But that night the writer was the only person she wanted to tell. In a phone booth inside the bar. A phone booth with strange faux gold paneling all over the door and walls. A little golden box. And she was drunk as a monkey. Little bleating voice of an operator. Little buzzings and ringings. Crackling. Then, *hello from America*, voice mail.

Later, they would argue, the photographer and the writer, about the girl in the photo. What about *her*? the writer demanded. What became of her? How could you leave her to fate? The words would sting the photographer's eyes and throat.

But in that booth, in that smoke-filled, not-American, crowded bar, she'd hit what was supposed to be the zenith of her career, and she felt . . . more empty than a shell casing. Having reached the only voice in the universe she ever loved—even just her voice-mail recording—all she could think was, What a voice. Even knowing there was no category for her love, or might never be back home in America, land of coupling, land of sanctioned marriage and two-person twined knots, land of tireless good-citizen living, land of the happy family, land of the free and the brave and the locked imagination, land of ignorant homeowner masses lined up in twos. Why can't I just be gay, her head went, or why can't we just live with the people we love and not worry about the sex, or why is sex such a big deal when it's so cluster-fucked anyway, her head tumbling thoughts until she was cross-eyed.

"I'm sorry," she said into the phone, and rang off.

As she moved back to her table of colleagues she thought, They will give her this. They will allow her this one night to act out. But tomorrow she will need the pumps and the black skirt and a crisp button-down white shirt, French or Italian, and her vinyl black hair captured in a tight ponytail. Because *The New Yorker* will be interviewing her by phone tomorrow. Because *Vanity Fair* will. All because of this award. *The* award.

I don't feel anything.

Remember what Virginia Woolf said: Give back the awards, should you be cleverly tricked into believing they mean something. Do not forget that the door you are being ushered through has a false reality on the other side. Do not forget that the door is opening only on someone else's terms, someone else's definition of *open*.

Then someone pulled her cheek and the whole table seemed to burst into whooping laughter, so she released her mind, these endless thoughts, and slid back into the booth.

This drunk successful woman making her choices.

She wanted to take her clothes off. She wanted to start a revolution. She wanted to give the prize back. Instead, she wiped her mouth to the recognition and celebration and alcohol, and with a great, swollen swagger she raised her glass and offered a wrong-mouthed toast:

Give me your tired, your poor,
Your huddled mazzes . . . yearning to breathe free,
The wrejjed refffff . . . use of your teeming shore,
Send these, the homeless, tempest-tozzedome,
I lift my lamp be(*burp*)zide the golden door.

There she was, a towering woman with people looking up at her, toasting her, a woman who had peed upright, a woman falling back into applause and laughter and adulation and dessert. Would it end there? Or would her momentum do what it does with drunk successful women, catapult her toward some man who would come inside her, an American six-footer maybe, between her legs as if her legs were meant for that opening up, her pussy meant for that entering, and all night inside her would he maybe say, You are so great, oh baby, god baby, you are greatness itself, yeah baby, let me give it to you, and would he? Give it to her? As if that's what she was made for, as if her body itself was brought to full height by the sexed-up flattery and hard prize of an American man?

Keep drinking.

The Poet

The poet is emerging from a dream. Her head on her desk, her eyes catching glimpses of things in retinal flashes, the crouch of unwritten words in her fingers.

She sees the world on its side, blurry and colored like waking is. She sees what must be the hairs of her own arm foresting up in front of her. She takes a deep breath, holds it, squints; the ordinary objects of the room keep their secrets a few seconds longer. She wets her lips with her tongue, which pulls her fully from sleep and activates the nerve-twine and vertebrae of her neck. She muscles up her biceps and *pop* she's awake.

She is in Prague. Her poet self brought her here. Prague: the way history stays alive in some cities: Art. Architecture. Absinthe. Sunflowers. Roads made from stones. She gazes out the frame of her window, sees the steeple of an eight-hundred-year-old church, mouths the word *psalm*. Pages of her own work rest under her arms, on the table, in view, urgent. She fingers through them. The sound of the paper is something like petrified wings.

She is in Prague working with another, more famous poet. In some older world, time, place, this would mean apprenticeship, would fall into an order, well placed. She has left America to position herself in a line with Eastern Europe, amid others trying to revive the buzz of history. World wars and hidden jars of honey. Night skies filled with sirens or people trying not to let their breathing sound. Sex under cover of bridges. The voices of writers exiled and humming like electricity.

But she stops being nostalgic. She knows she lives in this world, not some other, no matter how old and beautiful European cities are. She's an American poet in Prague.

She can afford to be. *Capitalist pig.*

She looks at the pieces of paper strewn around her: lines, scribbles, some words and pages barely decipherable. She picks up a half-eaten sandwich. Fuck it. She reaches over and pours an ounce of absinthe into a Pontarlier reservoir glass. The bulbous bottom swells with wet. Then she lays the flat, silver, perforated spoon across the rim and places a single cube of sugar on its face. She drips ice-cold purified water over the sugar until the color rises, until the gradual louche.

She lights a fire in the little room, sits in a hundred-year-old velvet chair. The heat brings on a dreamy glow of amber light. She drinks. Her hand moves to her other mouth, beginning the rhythmic throb. Because there is this: she'd rather live in the dreamy blur of everything she knows is dead than face the stark realism of an ordinary hand at the turn of this stupid-ass century. What a dull turning it's turning into.

With her want she makes a decision: tonight she will abandon the prestigious workshops and seek out live porn. It is easy to make a clean exit when you are unburdened by relationships.

In the not-American night she is partly her poet self and partly her id. She passes a man near a bar who says something ludicrous to her. She doesn't respond. Most of the time she's either in her mind or in her body—thinking or acting. She doesn't talk much. Never has.

She is aware of three things: the bruise-black effect of the night in the corridors of this city; her feet and their syncopated physicality; and the street itself.

A pounding between her legs.

She drains a flask from the inside pocket of a black leather jacket. She has been given the address to a place where a woman might mouth the mouths of other women.

What she wants first is to watch. To watch two women, not American, bring themselves to the brink of animal. The cum, the piss, the shit. Blood and sweat and mouths and salt. Skin reddened or scraped or bleeding or bitten or bruised. *Shoved.*

That violence.

Then she wants to dominate the scene.

If the scene fails, the writing will.

Of course she finds what she wants.

She purchases what she wants, gives herself exactly what she wants. She gives it and gives it until the having of it becomes the word *mine*, and beyond that even, until her thinking and her physical responses obliterate each other.

The poet watches from a velvet chair. A Moroccan, her skin black as oil, is fisting a Pole. The Pole is blindfolded, and her arms are bound to her sides with heavy white hang-yourself rope. She is on the marble floor of a large, high-ceilinged flat. Her legs are spread so wide she looks as if she might dislocate at the hips.

The Moroccan's ass is high up in the air and her pussy and asshole are alive, opening and closing alongside her labor. She works hard on the Pole, her blue-black arm disappearing into the white.

Make her red and swollen, the poet says. She sits with her legs crossed, breathing calmly, her hands clasped beneath her chin. A delicate glass of absinthe on the table next to her.

The fisting of the Pole extends over time in waves.

When the poet is satisfied at the raw cleft of the Pole, she instructs the Moroccan to stop. The Pole's breathing heaves; spit slides from her parted lips. Red blotches bloom on her white skin, randomly, the colors of the Polish flag. Her lips more than swollen.

The poet carefully opens a prepared towel, revealing a row of syringes with fingertip-size blue caps. She sits back down, tells the Pole to keep her legs spread. *Don't move. If you move or make a sound, it will be the death of you.* Then, after a pause: *Go on, then.*

The Moroccan takes one needle and removes the blue cap. She crouches over the Pole with the intensity and concentration of a doctor. The Moroccan's biceps flex as she moves in. She pierces the Pole's inner thigh, close to her pussy, in a place where blue veins river-shudder beneath the infant-thin skin. Down first, pressing her finger at the skin firmly, then up, making a stitch. The Pole's skin quivers but she does as she is told, does not move her body. She swallows a moan. The Moroccan caps the little needle and chooses another.

A small dot or two of blood emerges like the red head of a pin on a world map.

And again.

With each needle the Pole's breathing deepens and heavies.

Sweat forms quickly on her upper lip, her cheeks, her stomach, her inner thighs.

The poet almost feels the Pole's increasing light-headedness. The dizzy rise from pain to the rush of endorphins, the delirium at the top, the uncanny wish for more, even as a blackout seems imminent.

Twenty little needles up one thigh, twenty little needles down the other, blue caps creating railroads across the territory of a woman's body.

The Pole's toes shake like someone hanged.

The Pole clenches her teeth now and again.

Drools.

Still, she makes no sound.

Her hair flowing out from her head like a sunflower.

Her beating heart, to the dictatorial eye of the poet, is as stunning as a Warsaw uprising. How glorious the nearly silent criminal adventure.

Later, after each needle is removed, after the Pole is carefully wiped with antiseptic and given water and a loving warm hand bath by the naked poet and the Moroccan, after she is double body-cradled and sung to and rocked, all three women fuck the night into dawn, trading powers and alliances, surrendering or annihilating without attention to origin or plan. There is blood from more than one body. Mouths attack and retreat. Bruises rise like bomb blasts. Hands and fingers disappear into tunnels and caves. There is piss and cum and tears. Smears of shit make new symbols on the sheets. The sounds coming from the room would be intolerable to anyone on the outside, were it not for the fact that the lodgings are bought and paid for.

Then, after, she sleeps like a baby, heaped there with them on a bed made from women without rules.

She wakes with her face nearly smothered between two swollen breasts—Polish, whiter than white. The other body spoons her from behind—African Moroccan, so black it is blue. She is between nations. The salt and stick of cum between her legs smears across her thighs and ass and on her cheek and shoulders. A streak of blood near her mouth, the taste of metal. The scent of the inside of women is pungent and loud even inside her breathing. She licks her teeth and opens her mouth as if to speak, but she is not speaking.

It is the silence before the line.

Briefly she wants to linger there. Maybe she wants to die there. Then not. She gets out of bed, stumbling like a drunk morning-after man. She looks and looks and finds nothing, no pen, no pencil. Where the fuck is anything? Where the fuck is she? Right. Not her own room.

A purse on the floor.

She rummages through it. Women shit. Kohl eyeliners—

penlike. Paper? Nothing nothing nothing. She scans the room in that way that eyes work in the early morning, meaning not much, malfunctioning lenses.

Pillowcase.

And thus she begins, the first line already bursting toward rupture in her brain, what other people would call a hangover or the cusp of a migraine. She nearly barfs before she can get it down:

This impression I could ravish us/this blood-bodied pang

Her phone rings. She holds it to her ear.

The difference between a sentence and a line.

The writer has been hospitalized again, says the voice. She has stopped eating, speaking, everyone has gathered there at the hospital. Won't she, please, *come*?

History and time open like a mouth, inside which pulses the small pang of an ordinary woman.

The Playwright

Why is everything in hospitals the color of mud or mold? The playwright stops typing for a second and stares at his hands on his laptop. He can't believe he's already writing this. Already twisting it into art. *Cannibal.* He feels a pang of guilt. *You're in a hospital. Your poor sister is dying.* But even as his heart is beating him up in his chest, he can't not do it. He can't. He looks up at the strange and sporadic rivulet of people coming by to see his sister: former students, acquaintances, colleagues, fans of her books. It's a pitch-perfect humanity parade. If he doesn't get it down right now, it will blur and hum away like a train.

She'd be on his side. Wouldn't she?

Then again, she's dying. That's what they're all so somber about. When they spot him in that Naugahyde chair, hunched over a laptop, they must think he's odd. But there is a profound sibling secret, like a spider's thread, from his body to hers: No one knows more about the death in life and life in death than he and his sister. Their family a war zone. He breathes the artificial air. *God, this place smells like someone shit antiseptic.*

When they were children, he used to make his sister play Romeo and Juliet with him. Love scenes and death scenes from the play, which he'd been assigned in school. Though she was only six at the time, and he fifteen, he reconfigured his sister into a Romeo. Green leotard tights and a black down ski vest. He even cut her hair in what he considered an Elizabethan style, much to his mother's dismay, and talked her into a small codpiece he'd made from a sock. He taught her many of Romeo's lines to Juliet—*let lips do what hands do—wherefore art thou*—kid sisters were like chimps, you could get them to mimic anything. Her adoration knew no bounds. He'd stand at the top of the stairs, his sister at the bottom, all her longing in words and body reaching upward to him.

She was good.

Although no one, in any production he'd seen since—in Central Park, London, L.A., Venice—had been a finer, more beautiful, bath-towel-for-hair-hanging-past-his-ass Juliet than he'd been, in his mother's silk robe.

But during one of their private performances, when he was sixteen and she was seven, his sister did the unthinkable: she improvised a line. *Pity the small backs of children,* he heard her saying. *They carry death for us the second they are born.* They gazed at each other with a heavy stillness, then, his Juliet at the top of the carpeted stairs, her Romeo holding his hand out and up toward her, like faith.

"That's not your line," he said.

"But it is," she'd said. "My line." And she'd grabbed at her codpiece and thrown it to the shag carpet. It was their last performance together. Something was shifting, he remembers thinking. She was acting more like Hamlet than Romeo.

He can see her clearly now, in his mind's eye. Was she a writer even then, his sister? At six, seven years old? Some strange prodigy primate taking form underneath him?

Sometimes it feels as if he can't exit the family drama he left when he was sixteen. Or *thought* he left.

His skin itches. Doesn't it? He scratches his own wrists three times. Six. Nine. He knows exactly what the itching is. He feels all wrong, away from the calm and the cedar-soap smell of his lover's skin, the ground wire of his voice. He can feel his own internal organs lurching, especially his lungs and heart and possibly his prostate. Can one feel one's prostate? He takes a deep breath. Holds it for three seconds. Blows it back out, pacing his breathing. He does it three times. He hears his lover's voice: *You need to self-soothe. Self-soothe! Self-soothe.*

He closes his eyes. He sees his lover's body in the dark of their penthouse bedroom. New York City night light—the moon, the windowed eyes of adjacent buildings, neon signs and street traffic glow—illuminates the terrain of his lover's body: the top of a shoulder, the hill of a hip, his hair like a forest of wood shavings. He can smell the skin of his lover. He breathes him. *Cedar-scented soap cedar-scented soap cedar-scented soap.*

The only calm he has ever known has come from this: a man loving a man in the face of this city, in a room lit by night and skin. Why can't he always feel like this? He grinds his teeth exactly three times. Every other moment of his life, his ordinary life, ordinary days and hours and weeks and the ever-excruciating ticking and grating of time and tasks and human pretenses, feels to him like a series of chops. Like a carrot cut quickly on a wooden block. He hears the *chop chop chop* in threes. He doesn't want to leave this room. He doesn't want to feel anything outside this room. He wills the chopping sound to stop by breathing in cedar and skin. The chopping sound melds with someone's heels on linoleum.

His sister. He keeps his eyes closed. Sister. Simultaneous lifeline, loveline, and yet stone to the bottom of everything.

An alarm goes off in the distance. Some other hallway. *Code blue*. Some shuffle of scrubs. "Death is a body everywhere," he types onto his laptop. Then deletes it. Then retypes it. Deletes. Until it's just the word *death* staring at him.

Being on the West Coast makes him feel homicidal. That's just true. Part of him thinks, Well then, go ahead and die already, my sister, my imperfect other, it's astonishing we made it this far. You deserve it. Rest. Some other part of him bitch-slaps the first. *Vulgar. Insensitive. Asshole.* What kind of brother thinks a thing like that?

He retunes his ears to the scene around him. His fingers then flurry. He can't stop typing. Typing everything the visitors, orderlies, doctors, nurses around him in the hospital-hell hallway are saying to each other. He just can't not do it.

He sighs. He hates hospitals. Well, everyone does, but his hatred has a locus, an image arrested from the past.

His sister, as a girl of eight, on her stomach in a hospital bed. Her blood blooming up red from below, staining the white of the sheets, staining the word *daughter* with *father* and *family*. Blooming from her injuries. A paternal rape gone so badly wrong they had to keep her on her stomach.

He looks over toward his sister's room, then back across the waiting room at the performance artist. The only other permanent member of the tribe. His suspicions tug at him. He narrows his eyes at her. She chews her fingernail to the quick. One side of her hair is neon blue, the other bruise blue. How old is she, even?

Where's the filmmakerhusbandbrotherinlaw?

He stands up. He passes the performance artist in silence, walks to his sister's door. He steps in, out, in, out, and then in. He crosses the linoleum floor, avoiding tiny fissures. He reaches out, across the antiseptic air and beeping monitor, and holds her hand. The hand of a writer and the hand of a playwright and the silence between them.

She's a caterpillar in a cocoon. His mind goes slack and gentle. Her body is emaciated. Studying the blue veins in her eyelids and wrists, he recalls the primal scene which separated them—his boyman self on the cusp confronting his father with the truth of his assault—how he'd brought a knife, he'd meant to stick it into his father's gut as hard as he could, but his father had quickly overpowered him—his father the brute, his father the big-bodied masculine animal—his father then knifing his mouth wider, the blood shooting up and then pooling around his teeth and tongue.

His mother a useless blur in the hallway. His sister under the bed, eyes pleading.

Later, he had his mouth repaired, in the same hospital where his sister had lingered between life and death, after the push and cut of father. And yet, the next day, even knowing what it meant to his sister, he—*the words slow down in his head*—

Left.

Her.

There.

It was the last time he saw her.

It's a terrible love he carries. His guilt keeping the distance between them, East Coast and West. His guilt driving him to be the New York playwright, the star, the success. The bad brother. The toast of the town. The great gay playwright and the penthouse that he built. The abandoning one. The one who left her to the wolves.

He opens his mouth and whisper-speaks to his sister between the pulses of the heart monitor. "Where are you?" He stares at their hands. Everything they are now is in their hands. He puts his head down. He kisses her hand once, twice, three times. The magic of fairy tales and children. She doesn't stir. People don't know anything about love. It's nothing, they told us. *Fate moves over the small backs of children. They carry death for us the second they are born.*

He returns to the hallway, pacing in and out and in and out and in and out of the doorway. He sits back down. Back to his laptop, he registers the performance artist's Where-the-hell-have-you-been looks, but ignores them.

What is she doing here, anyway? Perched with her knees up, scowling at everyone who comes by? Pieces of words now like glimpses float in the hospital corridor: "I wonder if I can donate blood while we are here" and "I'd die for a vanilla latte but all they have here is sludge water" and "Yeah, five-thirty A.M., isn't that the crack of shit? I hate getting up early but we have rehearsals in the basement of a free clinic and we can only use it before they open or after they close . . ."

But then, suddenly, everyone around him stops their ambient babble.

The playwright looks up from his typing. The hospital people aren't saying anything. Why aren't they saying anything? He closes his laptop, gets up. An orderly walks by him with a tray of hot towels. He grips his own biceps, too hard. He grabs the fabric of his own shirt. The performance artist is the only other person in the room who is directly involved. He clears his throat and asks her where the filmmaker is.

The performance artist looks up with the slowness of a neon Lorax. "He said he needed to walk around."

"Listen," the playwright says, rubbing the back of his neck in little three-circle massages. "Do *you* understand what happened? Because that story they told me on the phone is nonsense. Tell me any details you know. Tell me what the doctors are saying. She looks unbelievably pale. Her skin looks as thin as a communion wafer."

The performance artist sits mute and still. She looks to him like fatigue dumped a load of human in a hallway, like refuse. *Can a person die of inside-hospital ennui?*

"I bet you get a performance out of this," he says.

"Yeah? And what the hell would that look like?"

In the urban dictionary next to the word *emo* is this girl. "Well," he persists, "you know, there's a Beckett play. It's called *Happy Days*. There's a woman in it named Winnie, who gets buried in mud. Up to her breasts."

"You don't say." The performance artist eyes the elevator.

"Yes, but we never learn how she got buried."

"Fascinating." The performance artist gnaws at a new finger.

"Or trapped."

She chews her fingernails.

"What's he done? Becker? Anything on streaming?"

"*Beckett*. Samuel." Briefly he wants to slap her into womanhood.

Mercifully, the elevator makes a holy *ding* and the filmmaker enters stage left. The playwright walks—nearly hopping—twelve steps in sets of threes to meet him.

He touches the filmmaker's arm—Jesus, this guy is big. I mean, nothing he didn't know, but Jesus. He could do some damage with those cannons. He pulls the filmmaker aside, whispery, needy, as if they're guy pals or comrades or anything but what they are: the brother who abandoned her and the husband who can't cope with her descent. "Just give it to me straight, no chaser. What's going on? Really."

The filmmaker's skin looks blue-gray and heavy mugged. "She's . . . I don't know how to answer that. None of this makes any sense." His eyes are marbled in hues of hazel specked with brown.

"Well, what was the instigating event? All they're telling me is that she suddenly went deaf and dumb, and went on some kind of Kafkaesque hunger strike." He swallows, trying to lower his voice an octave.

"One morning she seemed a little distracted. Staring at the wall. That's all. I said, 'Baby, are you okay?' She turned to me and smiled. We kissed. I went to work. So did she, I assume. I assume the day was like any other day—it rained, she taught her classes and I taught mine, neighborhood dogs barked, the mail came. I came home that night, she was on the floor. Unconscious." The filmmaker draws a breath, sucking oxygen like a human vacuum.

"She just dropped? Just like that?" *Don't say DEAD don't say dropped DEAD don't say DEAD.* The playwright's sphincter twitches. His lover's voice in his head: *Be aware of social codes be aware of social codes be aware.* But it's not working, the hallway lights of the hospital are too bright, the filmmaker is so physical, he's like walking physicality, and the playwright's longing to write it all down is creeping up on him, like it always does, like black letters and words growing larger and larger until they're walking around on the white floor before his eyes, big as people, the word DEAD bigger than any, with cartoon-muscled arms and shoulders.

"Yeah. Look, I don't really want to talk about this right now." The filmmaker closes his eyes and rubs at them with his thumbs.

"Okay, yeah. Of course. I'm going to see if I can find a doctor to talk to me."

"You know what?" the filmmaker nearly shouts. "You do

that. You get a doctor to talk to you. I'm sure you New York people deal with this stuff all the time, right? Depression? Neuroses? Pathologies? You want to know what they'll say? They're gonna tell you the same story they told me. They're going to tell you *there's nothing wrong with her.* She's a goddamn physical specimen. See how far that gets you."

"Nothing wrong with her." The playwright starts ticking the fingernails on his thumb and forefinger in sets of threes.

"Look, I'm sorry," the filmmaker says. "I told you, it's hard for me to talk about this right now. I haven't slept much, and my kid is with my mother . . ." His hands knot themselves into fists. Dangling fists with nothing to do.

"You got it. Not another word out of me." But the playwright is lying. He suddenly feels a sense of thrilling danger. Several sentences line up in his mouth. He bites the inside of his cheek.

But then comes another menacing *ding*, and the elevator door opens again, wide as a fucking mouth.

There he is, Mr. Asshole. The painter, the exiled ex-husband, the walking ego with a ready dick. Who the hell invited him?

The performance artist stands up. The filmmaker has his back to the elevator, so he doesn't see the painter until he realizes the room has gone quiet again. The playwright feels coiled, urgent, ready to lash.

"What, did somebody die in here? You all look like fucking corpses." The painter, laughing his ass off. Stale booze fills the air.

The performance artist flushes in the face like she's eaten niacin; she puts her hand up like a stop sign and closes her eyes.

The playwright counts to three; he can feel the action before it happens.

The filmmaker, now husband, he's turning, turning, he sees the painter, until one man faces the other.

The filmmaker throws an exquisite left hook and drops the painter to the floor.

Blood mouth-splatters across the linoleum.

Orderlies rush in like moths.

Then, in three seconds that feel more like minutes, the playwright snaps out of it, rushes over to the filmmaker, grabs his big-ass arm, and ushers him out of the building. No sense in anyone getting arrested right now. He hurries the filmmaker through an EXIT door into a stairwell, down and down and down until they reach the parking lot.

There, in the lot, things slow back down to human speed. They walk to the filmmaker's car like two men walking, though one of them is counting steps. He can still feel the filmmaker's rage. *If I die at the hands of this man in a parking garage, in some ways it will be a fitting end.* Dying, finally, in his sister's moment of peril.

They arrive at the door of the filmmaker's car. The filmmaker opens his mouth again, then closes it. The playwright touches his shoulder. "Look, you just go home now. Try to get some rest. I'll call you if there's any change. Just get out of here for a little while. You need a break." He has no idea where this modulated voice comes from, but he suspects he's channeling his lover. *Have empathy for others have empathy for others have empathy. Even if you have to pretend at first.* Is he pretending?

The filmmaker drives away, taillights illuminating the exit. The playwright makes his way back up the stairwell from the parking lot in steps of threes.

Back in the hospital hallway, the painter is now upright in a chair, hurling slurry, hushed obscenities into the dead white hallway. "*Cocksucking motherfucker* . . ." The playwright touches touches touches his own elbows as he crosses the room and takes a seat.

Settling in with his laptop, he looks at them—the painter and the performance artist—and he sees it: She's here for *him*. Not for his sister. She knew he'd show up.

Just look at them. They're like a human West Coast tableau. Like scraps of indigo and blood-colored glass, foreign money, vintage jewelry and hip little buttons, hair art, toy soldiers and firecrackers and pieces of wire and bullet casings and the feathers of birds, the bones of animals, a half-smoked joint and a bunch of foreign beer caps and Dunhill butts. The look like they should be at Jim Morrison's grave. Père Lachaise. Drinking Courvoisier. The painter takes out a flask. The playwright smirks.

Who are we in moments of crisis or despair? Do we become deeper, truer selves, or lift up and away from a self, untethered from regular meanings like moths suddenly drawn toward heat or light? Are we better people when someone might be dying, and if so, why? Are we weaker, or stronger? Are we beautiful, or abject? Serious, or cartoon? Do we secretly long for death to remind us we are alive?

He shivers. What the hell was that about? Was that his sister's voice, or his? He claps three times and says, "Okay, people—you're not the center of the universe here, right? Everybody get a *grip*." He walks over to the pile of performance artist and painter. "We shouldn't all be trying to stay here this way. It's not helping her. It's pathetic. Look what comes of it. We should just take shifts. Come tell me your work"—he glances at the performance artist—"or *whatever*, schedules. I'll call everyone. I'll make a visitation chart."

But that's not what he's typing.

He's typing out stage directions.

A doctor steps into the room, as if on cue.

Nightmaking

In her sleep, the night sky stitches a story through the girl.

Her brother is a fox pup chasing a mouse over a snow-covered field. The fox pup leaps straight up into the air where the mouse tracks end and plunges nose first into the blanket of white. The fox emerges and shakes its head to free the snow from its fur. The fox is laughing. A mouse in its mouth.

Her mother is a moon eye in the sky. Not perfectly white, but bruise-hued. The moon eye casts a gaze over all of the world, over violence and lovers with equal compassion, over living and dead, over children and old men curling into brittle-boned fetal positions in bed, curling around what used to be their wives, taking their last breaths, over chickens and badgers and snakes and trees, over rivers and rocks and breath.

Her father is not a tree.

Let all the other fathers before hers be trees.

Her father is a door.

Anywhere.

Anytime.

Opening or closing, depending on the story and the girl's place in it.

The Filmmaker

The filmmaker is beating a heavy bag to death.

Having recently clocked the painter, he finds that slamming the heavy bag feels more satisfying. In the backyard behind his house, at night, his blows land and thud. He pictures the chest and gut of a man. Fisted speed dug deep from a bellyful of rage and jabs extended until they're shot-strung back to the shoulder. Again. Again. The throbbing sound so familiar he doesn't recognize it. Comforting.

It's what he knows how to do in the face of inertia.

What if a man's body is all that drives action, and not the stupid heart?

Anything but the heart.

So he beats the holy hell out of this simulacral man in the backyard for hours, until he's spent, until he's just a man bent over and panting. His breath fogs before him in the cold night. It seems good that he can't kill the heavy bag. He hangs his head. This is killing him. No, not killing him. But it is some kind of crucible he doesn't understand.

His wife. How can there be nothing he can do to fix it? It makes him want to hit things as hard as he can.

He looks at the back of his house. It stares dully back at him. Wifeless. Sonless. Without life. He goes inside, and when he looks back through the window to the backyard, all he sees is black, like the screen before the film begins, the moon a white projector's beam.

This is the first night in seven he has come home from the hospital. It's the only respite he has given himself. A night to fight and release the chemical chaos of things. Without turning any lights on, he walks through the kitchen, opens the refrigerator, removes a Newcastle beer, twists the cap off, drinks most of it standing in the fluorescent glow. Then he removes his Everlast workout gloves, carefully unwraps his hands, the black bands falling to the floor like tired-out snakes. They sting from the gap between cold night air and warm domesticity.

He grabs another beer, then walks through the dark and lifeless house to his wife's writing room. He stands in front of her bookshelves. He stares at the shelf of her own books, books written by her. The beer going down his throat branches out across his chest. His throat is warm. His hands ache. Their lives together make a list in his skull, because that's all he's able to think or feel.

Before she was a writer, she was an abused daughter.

Before he was a filmmaker, he was a neglected son.

Before he turned to art, he was a bouncer at a casino.

Before she turned to art, she was a flunking-out addict.

Both of them briefly arrested and incarcerated.

Both of them stealing their lives back, pursuing lives of the mind. Both of them carrying invisible injuries, injustices, betrayals, all in silence.

When they first met, he took her to Gold's Gym. Taught her how to box, how to defend herself, stayed with it even when she accidentally punched herself in the nose. She took him to a swimming pool to do laps, because she said water was the one place she felt free, and he swam laps even though he was allergic to chlorine.

She introduced him to the movies *Cool Hand Luke* and *On the Waterfront*.

After the gym, he played Bach for her on the cello.

It was as if the crappiness of both their lives opened up and let them at each other.

Before they were anyone, they were who they would become in each other's arms, each of them passing through crucibles to reach the other, each of them arriving at art instead of death.

She writes stories of their lives and desires and fears.

He makes art films based on the stories.

She collects experiences and images and pulls them down to the page.

He takes actions and images and projects them up onto a screen.

Who are they? What is their love? Is it their son? Is it their art?

He touches the spines of her books in the dark.

Love isn't what anyone said. It's worse. You can die from it at any moment.

He picks out a book she wrote, containing one of the stories he adapted to film. The film is nearly finished. The closing scene is her. She is walking naked toward the angry ocean on a cold day in November. Her blond hair wrestles the wind. She keeps walking even after she is knee-high in waves. He knew, as he filmed her, that the water was freezing. He also knew she wouldn't flinch. She walked far enough to dive straight into the oncoming waves, the camera trained on her, their son perched in a carrier on his back. And then she swam against the waves. Bold strokes into white-frothed swells. Far enough that he screamed, "Cut!" Far enough that he stopped filming. Far enough that he started to yell into the wind and the noise of the surf—it was a cold day, no one else around on the beach—"*Stop! Come back!*" Her name, but his voice was swallowed by gales and tides. His chest tightening. His thoughts racing as his body readied itself for action: *Set the child on the shore remove your boots remove your jacket and pants enter the ocean for her even though you are a weak swimmer enter the ocean for her do not watch her disappear into water.* Their son's voice behind his head a cooing sound, "Mama," as he reached for the strap at his shoulder.

But she did stop.

He saw her turn back to look at them, the way a seal's head pokes up sporadically to eyeball a human on shore.

And then she swam back to them.

She left the water cold and shivering, and he wrapped her in a towel, and she said to him plainly and without the suggestion of drama, “Did you get the shot? Was it okay?” Her lips blue, even as she smiled, a little like a corpse mermaid.

Is their love their art? Are their lives making art?

He stares at the spines of the books in her writing room. He feels she is the other side of things—the balance, the space to his motion, velocity, force. If in him need drives the fist, then in her space receives all action. But it is not a velvety romantic love. It is creative and destructive. He thinks of her body. He wants to fuck the room of her. The whole house.

Suddenly he needs to be in the bedroom. He makes his way upstairs, into the higher-sexed place of their marriage. In their bedroom he sees deep burgundy and indigo sheets in wrestled piles on the bed. He can smell their sex. Dead candles, waiting for dusk and sex, hide in the shadows. On the wall above where her sleeping head should be there are black-and-white photographs of . . . what? Him and his wife. Right? Taken by their photographer friend, lovingly. Right? He pauses and his eyes fall on them, on their revelation, on their presence. Two-dimensional selves in giant oak frames, perfectly square. The photo of her: wife half underwater, half surfaced, seal-like and caught off guard. Her hair splayed out like seaweed. The photo of him: a fighting scene, his own arm extending mid motion in blur, half his face in the frame, half not, the object of the blow entirely out of the shot. He looks at the two images, caught there like that above the world of the bed, and wonders what he is really looking at. Is it true? His chest hurts some. He steadies himself by sitting on the edge of the bed.

His hands rummage around in the bedside table drawer. He isn't looking. He's feeling. The aqua glass pipe finds his hand. And the pot inside a plastic bag, just like in anyone's house. The perpetual life of the lighter finding his fingers. In this way he is able to breathe like a normal fucking man again. He fills his lungs with haze and lift and the promise of the rational mind's loosening. He misses his son. His body aches for his wife. Thoughtless and animal heavy. *Come home*, he thinks, like a mantra. *Swim home.*

Alone, in their house, without her, he does what men do when they are not crying. He puts his beautifully violent face in his own hands and hangs his head and his shoulders heave. Something like silent pantomime crying. And then it breaks through him, guttural sounds, and then the sounds grow into moans and then he's throwing the glass pipe at the photo of himself and shattering glass all over the place. Goddamn it. Nothing nothing nothing but this: he cannot save her, fix her, *make it right.* There is nothing he can do but love his son and love his wife and wait. He sits up on the edge of the bed.

What is a man without action?

He drops his head, defeated.

That is when he sees it, down beyond his scabbed and roughened hands resting on his thighs, past his battered knees balling up in front of him, all the way down to his feet planted helplessly there on the hardwood floor. The edge of a book jutting out quietly from beneath the bed. Without thinking he reaches down and picks it up. It is not a published book, like the rows and rows that fill their home. It is not one of her books, and yet it is most definitely her book. It is a book people write in when they mean for it to be kept out of the world. It is a journal. Its cover burnished red and worn. A leather strap wrapped and wrapped around it. A pen periscoping up from the top.

Quietly as a child he opens the book, looks at pages randomly. Flipping through. Her novel. The one she's writing . . . was writing. Pieces of stories, little drawings and notes, and whole pages of narrative. He stops on a page and starts to read, with only the moon for light:

The Girl

You must picture your image of Eastern Europe.

In your mind's eye.

Whatever that image is.

However it came to you.

Winter.

That white.

One winter night when she is no longer a child, the girl walks outside, her shoes against snow, her arms cradling a self, her back to a house not her own but some other. It is a year after the blast that has atomized her entire family in front of her eyes. It is a house she has lived in with a widow woman who took her in—orphan of war, girl of nothingness. . .

He stops reading for a minute. He feels like he knows the girl. He feels like he can see her. Has he read this before? No, that's impossible. He looks down again and reads on, and in the reading he begins to see images in frames:

On the ninth day the widow takes the food straight to the girl. She squats down on the ground. The girl immediately starts to point to her creations and name them. The woman nods. They eat carrots. When the girl is finished naming, the woman points to a smooth blue-gray stone, which seems to inhabit a forest of sticks.

Vilkas, the girl says.

Wolf.

On the tenth day the girl finishes the city and enters the widow's house.

Inside, the house is filled with books and photographs. Books and books from all places and all times. Old history books with spines reddish brown like old blood, more recently published books with the sheen and glow of the West. Oversize books and palm-size books, every color imaginable, titles filling the room like voices. Books and photographs, more books and photographs than dishes or furniture. Photographs of Paris and Germany, of America, Poland, Prague, Moscow. Photographs of crowds in squares, their coats and hats testaments to cold, photos of farmers and villagers, their faces plump and red as apples as they break from the fields for something to eat and drink. Photographs of animals caught entering or emerging from the forest, their animal faces wary and low to the ground, their animal eyes marking the distance between species. Books and photographs of trees and houses and festivals, of musicians and artists and mothers, of statesmen and children, of soldiers and guns and tanks and bodies and snow made red. Books and books about art. Photographs of the widow. Of her hands. Her cheek and hair. The white of her collar and the nape of her neck. Photos taken by her husband who was arrested, beaten, and stolen away to a Siberian prison.

The widow broken by loss and the girl with the blown-to-bits family begin to live together in this house made of art.

This house made of art.

His heart is pounding. His head is pounding. No—it's the door. It's someone at the front door. At first he's frozen, stuck in the snow-covered story of a girl inside the words of his wife. Then he's back in his own house in the dark. He tucks the journal underneath an arm and moves toward sound and action.

Moving Action

It's the poet. At the door. The filmmaker can see her face through the thick-paned glass. He opens it. The night air nearly snaps his psyche in two.

She rubs her cropped thatch of hair and the leather of her black biker jacket makes an ache sound.

He embraces her. The hug is awkward, the journal still under his arm. The poet's body feels to him like it is alive in a way that his is not. Like she's filled with current.

The poet twitches away from him, and moves into the house. "Are you going to turn a light on, or do you just want to sit in the dark like we're in a movie?" she says.

"Sorry. I'm just . . ."

"Exhausted?"

The filmmaker turns on a lamp. The room honeys-over in hue. He goes into the kitchen to retrieve his wife's bottle of Balvenie scotch. He hands the bottle to the poet. She thanks him, then proceeds to drink straight from the bottle. He sees her neck screen size: the muscles are filmable, her head tilted back and back in the way of a real drinker. He likes her masculinity. They get along.

She stares at the thick of him. "Would you like to just sit here together, or do you feel like talking?" She pulls a fattie and a lighter out of her black leather jacket pocket, wets it between her lips, lights up, and hands it to him.

He doesn't say anything, but he holds it up between them with a quizzical look on his face that asks, *Customs?*

She shakes her head. "Got it on this side. The orderly was holding."

He's glad she's here. The poet on their couch across from him, as if things were the way they're supposed to be.

"We have to *do* something," she says. Her words echo through his body.

The filmmaker smashes his empty beer bottle onto the coffee table in front of them. The sound tightens the cords in the poet's neck and jaw, but she doesn't flinch.

Silence.

The filmmaker sets the journal down on the table as if this whole night is moving normally. How does anyone survive any relationship? How does anyone move through humans without killing them, or themselves?

The two of them stare at the object.

"Yeah. I don't know," the filmmaker says. "This is hers. I don't know if there's anything in there that matters. I don't even know why I'm telling you this."

"Lemme see it." The poet holds out her hand.

The filmmaker opens the journal to the part he was reading before and hands it to the poet. He puts his head in his hands, for he feels as if it might sever from his neck at any moment. Partly he wishes it just would. The second the poet's voice begins, the writer's story rises up to them something like heat does, invisible and under the spell of physics. She reads the writer's words aloud:

One day the girl is reading a poem in the widow's house. Next to the poem is a drawing of the poet: Walt Whitman. Next to the drawing the girl's imagination retrieves something it has not touched for a long while. A father. The girl's father before the blast was a poet. There. It is a thought, "father," it is the thought, "poet," and it does not kill her. The girl closes her eyes and fingers her tangles of blond hair and goes back, perhaps for the first time, to the memory of her father, her family before the blast.

Her father was a poet, her mother a weaver. Her father could engineer and build anything with only his hands, her mother could sing and make medicines and calm a child into dream—everything they were, happened between their hands. Her father taught her poems, and how to build a tiny city from mud and straw and twigs. Her mother taught her songs and how to make a pattern with cloth and color. And there was a brother. She lets the word become an idea. Brother. She remembers the touch of his hands. The warmth they shared when their cheeks met. How he smelled next to her before they drifted into sleep at night. Her mother the weaver. Her father the poet. Her other: brother.

She looks back at the image of Walt Whitman. She wonders, is a poet really a poet if his only songs are to his daughter, his wife, his son? If his extraordinary lyric merely puts children to sleep like moon whisper, or fills a house with star-shaped dreams? Is a poet a poet if there are no books that carry his words, his name, a drawing of his face?

She is the not-dead daughter of her father the poet.

In her memory she is four. She is on her father's shoulders in the darkened woods, next to a frozen lake. They skirt the woods without completely entering; forest animals scrutinize their movements. She is laughing, and that's how she remembers it: she is holding tight to her father's ears, he is saying, "Not so tight, my tiny, not so tight, you will pull your father's ears from his head!" Her laughter and his.

Is it love to want to die there, inside that image?

The not-dead daughter.

Later, her father creates an oral history of that moment, tells and tells it around great fires after dinners, after work, after the tiny family—a wife, a son, a daughter—has settled and touched one another and drunk and moved between house smells and fire. For something else happened there besides her love for him. Her knees pressed against his cheeks. A story. A story about animals.

"A caribou was walking against the forest next to a frozen lake with his family. The youngest fell lame and the mother,

who was already weakened from childbirth, insisted on carrying her. The mother became weaker and weaker, and at some point was so delirious with fatigue that she let slip the tiny life, into the great flattened white of things. A human girl and her father came upon the tiny thing just as it was dying. The girl held its head and the father sang a very old song with his eyes closed. It was what to do. Then she died."

And her father narrates the ending in song, lyric. But the girl's imagination . . . travels.

In her head, the girl continued her own story beyond the ending of the father and daughter who came upon the dying animal. In her story, the girl wonders, What was the last thing the youngest caribou saw? Was it the image of her animal father and her animal mother disappearing into blur and ice? Or perhaps by chance she saw her, her and her father, before she passed. If it was the strong back of her animal father and the tender rhythm of her animal mother's legs she saw, maybe her leaving took a home with it forever. And if it was the human father and daughter she saw last, perhaps the difference in their species melted as snow in a great thaw, the word she *and the word* her *becoming each other, daughter and caribou, perhaps their beating of hearts simply became the earth's cadence, perhaps bodies returned to their animal past—hand and hoof releasing to the energy of matter.*

She loves the story, this story her father told and told before her family was blown to bits—their bodies exploding back to molecules and light and energy. Fatherless, beautiful story poem.

It becomes a story she loves to death.
The not-dead daughter.
It is the story of children.

The poet puts the last of the joint out in the palm of her hand. "How long has she been writing this?"

The filmmaker answers, "About seven years."

But then the front door cracks open and the playwright flutters in like an enormous unstoppable moth. "Listen," he yell-breathes.

The filmmaker stands up.

"They said they . . . ," he sputters.

The filmmaker walks to the playwright and wordlessly grabs him by his arms, briefly lifting him slightly off the ground.

"They said they don't know if she will make it through the night. They're trying to determine if she took something. They won't know until morning. They said come back when the sun comes up. They said this should be over by then. One way or another." His words dissolve into breathing.

We have to do something.

The filmmaker lets go of the playwright and heads back out the front door, grabbing his car keys from a table. The front door swings behind him, open as a mouth.

The playwright stares at the poet, and at the broken glass, as they listen to the sound of a husband peeling out of his own driveway and neighborhood.

The poet cradles the writer's journal like a child.

The playwright holds his own arms. "What should we do?"

The poet stares past him into the night. Then she turns her gaze to the living room wall, there in the writer and filmmaker's house, the house where they've all come to know one another, the wall with the photo they've all seen.

She's thinking about grief and trauma, how they can hide out inside a woman, how they can come back.

The playwright follows her eyes, until he sees what she sees.

The photographer's framed image, the orphan girl lit up by the explosion, a girl blowing forward, a girl coming out of fire, a girl who looks as if she might blast right through image and time into the world

"I know what's happened," the poet says.

Expression

When the girl paints a red face, with orange streaks shooting from the eyes and mouth, the widow asks, "Is that your face? Are you angry?"

When the girl paints an indigo face, with aqua eyes and a green mouth, with hair like sea grass, the widow asks, "Is that your face? Are you swimming?"

When the girl paints a bright yellow face, with bright blue eyes and gold hair splaying out like the rays of the sun, the widow asks, "Is that your face? Are you happy?"

And when the girl paints a black face with a crimson gash interrupting the eye, the nose, the mouth, nearly dissecting the image, the widow asks, "Is that your face? Is that your fear?"

It is only when the girl paints a face that looks like a girl's, expressionless, flat, calm, just a girl looking out, not a smile but not the negation of one either, that the widow stops asking the girl about the faces. The widow smiles and hangs the painting of the quiet, calm girl on the wall in the common room.

The girl goes back to her labor. Every color alive.

Hundreds of faces on wood—as if a forest of faces could come alive.

The Painter

It's three A.M. He's thirsty. His jaw hurts where the fucking filmmaker tried to knock it off his face. He's lying next to the performance artist on a futon in her loft. She brought him home with her from the hospital, and not the first time. They've been doing it for years. The rest of the gang may have exiled him from their little posse, but not her. As long as he stays away from them, away from the woman who used to be his wife, there's not a goddamn thing they can say or do.

Whatever. He looks around the performance artist's room. She's snoring. He needs to not think. Badly. He reaches for a half-empty bottle of wine on the bedside table and drinks the rest in a single motion. He stares at the blank wall. He gets up. The naked man pads into the kitchen, finds another bottle of wine, opens it, brings it back to the bedroom. Drinks half. He rifles through some CDs there on the floor, finds *The Doors*. He sticks it in the CD player. Volume low. Sleeping, sexed-up woman. He finishes the bottle. He lies back down.

Resting there like a wetted corpse, next to this particular lover—who has always looked a little like a Nabokov nymphet to him, her pale taut skin, her pointy tits and hip bones, her girl-boy frame, one of those women with an eternally twelve-year-old body—he thinks of his life as a series of women's bodies. Women's bodies in every room he enters, every country, every gallery, every bar, every store or post office or restaurant. Married women and single women, professional women and working girls, women in therapy and women with money and women who barely spoke English, junkie women and artist women and famous women and skid-row women and all-used-up women and somebody's-daughter women. Women of every age. Riders on the storm. He drinks.

He has a memory of his ex-wife. The body of her, the devouring wife love hole. He thinks of the day he left her, remembers thinking something like, *It's easy.* I can leave the room, the house, the country. I can stop pretending to like Miles Davis and Nina Simone and Frida fucking Kahlo and Marguerite Duras. I can go to another house or state or country, and women who are not American might come sit on my face.

Faces are what he paints. Abstract faces, over and over and over again. He thinks of something someone said to him at his last show, entitled "I Am Cross with God: Intimate Portraits," a series of abstract faces, eight feet by eight feet. The person had said, "Why do the faces look like they are in pain?" It'd been half an hour into the opening, and he'd had seven glasses of wine. And he'd said back, "The next time you kiss someone you love, open your eyes. Think about what their face looks like. That close. That familiar. So familiar you can't bear it. Distorted." Then he walked away, grabbing two of the wine bottles on his way like a cowboy with a pair of revolvers.

His ex-wife's face comes again. But this memory, it's not like other people's memories. It's not a vision of the past. It's not a flashback. It's all inside a *now.* Because that's how he lives. Inside a now. Like dreams work. An image becomes a story becomes a life becomes a man and then it's now. The now of wine, the now of sex, the now of painting. So even though the now of her is far away, in a little white hospital room, he sees the used-to-be-them in a now.

The writer. The painter. She used to wear his pants. He used to wear her skirts. She had a half-shaved head. His hair went down past the middle of his back. She liked it in the ass. He liked it on his back. She made the money. He cooked the food. Still life with wife.

He sees his wife's face. In the kitchen of their then-house. He sees the features of her face, in color and brushstroke. He walks through their then-kitchen, out the back door, on his way to his backyard studio. She turns from the sink to say, "I love you." He thinks: How can you love me? That's some fucked-up love. That's mother love. Relentless and all-consuming. Then he thinks: love is an abstract word coming from a face hole.

In his mind's eye, then, her face becomes formless. He watches himself moving away, out of the wifehouse. Closing the door. Walking into the then-studio behind the house of her. Closing a second door. A room not the house, not her. A room of himself.

The room of his art. And then the image of his self overtakes all the images of women.

Inside the then-image of himself, he sits in his studio in the dark. His hand travels his face, a face unmade from the dark, the hand desiring, fingers longing for form. Five holes: Eyes. Nostrils. Mouth. His face. He has entered this room hundreds, perhaps thousands, of times. He always leaves as if he has fallen out of reality. What is a man in the face of art? A little cartoon.

He knows what is happening back inside the house. Inside the house it is night. Sitcoms and cable news and commercials repeat themselves aimlessly. People are dying, commentators narrating. Food sits hiding inside the dull hum of the refrigerator. Marriage objects make sounds and images: the refrigerator and stove and television and bed. Wifehouse. These thoughts are killing him. If he cannot eject them, he will die. Certainly he cannot paint with even their faintest echo in his mind.

In the then of him, he pulls a joint from his pocket, lights it blind. The end glows red for an instant as he inhales what he hopes will be a nothingness. Within seconds things get simpler. If he can just inhale the nothingness and dark around him and breathe out the light of the wifehouse behind him, he won't have to kill himself. Then he can turn the lamp on. Make his way to the table of brushes and thinner and linseed and tubes and layers of color more familiar than hands.

The ritual is always the same. Hours of pacing and lulling the skull to knock out the thinking. Going liquid. Wine. In bottles and jugs and half-filled jars. Wine and wine and wine and more wine. Lose the mind. Lose it. Jim Morrison. More wine.

Thought begins to leave, the joint diminishes to nothing, as if there is still a god, merciful and intimate. He waits for even his teeth to feel mysterious to him.

Comfortably lost inside this image of himself, he keeps following it. His then-self drinks a bottle of wine in about the time it takes to utter a few of her carefully crafted sentences. It pours down his chin and jaw. It burns a bit in his chest. He decides to remove all of his clothes. He squirts a wad of indigo into his palm. He crosses the room abruptly. Thoughtlessly. He assaults the canvas with a handful of indigo, mudlike. Then he retreats, returns to the table. He doesn't need to look down. His hands read like Braille the piles of tools and cylindrical thick tubes of color, the varying hairs of brushes, jars filled with thin liquid or liquid thick as the jelly of an eye, until his hand unburies a fat half-squeezed tube of onyx.

He consumes another half bottle of wine in the space of time most people would say they were considering an idea, or looking at an object with interest. He removes the pinch-small plastic white lid between thumb and forefinger, throws it on the floor with its fellow refuse. He fills the palm of his hand with onyx. Squeezes his two hands together. The room is a pierced aroma of turpentine, linseed, and pure color. He closes his eyes and paints his face. He smears out the searching of his eye valleys, makes a prayer shape around his nose, gives his mouth a wide black swipe. He stops. He has de-faced himself. He laughs. He drinks. Then he smears the color farther down his neck, to the bones between his shoulders.

This image of himself—it's turning him on in the present,

like it did in the past. Into this house we're born. Into this world we're thrown.

Reloading, his then-him hands move down his chest and gut in wild circles toward his dick. A face peering up, a single eye, grotesquely animal. He squeezes as if his dick were a tube of paint. A small ooze of fluid pearls up. He cups his balls. He squeezes another tube of paint and covers his cock, cool thick wet, and makes hand-dick friction sliding up and down, cold to hot. His hips are animal, his head is almost too heavy to hold up. His teeth clench his eyes close his skin sweats his spine nerve and muscle flex break down meaning. Near release he moves his free hand to his asshole and slides a painted finger inside himself. His ass makes sucking noises and his dick hand handles the coming sticking like oil and water, these fluids out of whack and slicked together. His asshole contracts in budding juiced thrusts until his cock, speechless, handless, faceless, dissolves into paint and cum.

His breathing slows. He reaches out to the painter's table and feels. A knife is closer to his hand than a brush. This is of no great consequence. He cuts. Not at the wrist. At his own jaw, from the ear down some, like a quote. Warm fluid eases in a stream down his neck, like the pool at the tip and the tiny stream down the shaft of his cock. His face is open. His mouth fills with saliva. His teeth calm and drown.

Then and only then does he move with real intention to the canvas. There is nothing wrong with this picture. There is nothing wrong with him. He presses himself against the canvas and pieces of a body smudge random chaotic forms onto white. He paints wildly, physically, with his body, his hands, brushes, oils, fluids, blood. For this is part of his claim to fame—his use of bodily fluids mixed with paint to paint giant abstract faces. He paints with the fluids of a self outside language and thought, he paints in barbaric attacks of color on the canvas of white—fight-back black or blood-born Alizarin crimson, Prussian blue, burnt sienna.

It is only inside abstraction and expression and chaos that he is alive.

In the vacuum left from his spent body, he has again painted an abstract face. Eight feet by eight feet. It might be a man's face and it might be a woman's face. Or both.

In the image of his past-him—he remembers—he passes out. But in his present he keeps watching that man all the way to morning.

Morning finds him smoking a cigarette, spent and hunched over and thoughtful. He's supposed to go back into the house. The house of the writer and the painter, husband and wife. Still life with wife. If he goes back inside the house, he thinks, he will die. It doesn't matter what love is. If it even exists. If he goes back inside domesticity, he will die. For him it's this: wife or death.

In the image of the then-him, he stubs out the cigarette and pinches the skin at the cut near his jaw until it bleeds. He half-assedly wipes himself down with a hundred turpentine wipes and puts his clothes back on. His skin stings like fuck. He looks like he's been in some kind of fire or explosion. If he lit a match right now, he'd burst into flames. He bites the cork out of a jug of wine, holds its mouth to his, and drinks. He tastes blood and wine. He wishes its mouth would drown his. Tears happen hot. Then evaporate against his turpentine skin.

That is when it happens. He looks at the painting of the face. It might be a man's face and it might be a woman's face and it might be both. He walks not back into the house, but to the car. He drives not to the store, not to some familiar and ordinary place in their lives, not the corner bar, not the park, not the hills. He drives downtown and gets out of the car and walks to the door of the apartment of a woman less than half his age, half his life. He knocks on her door with his wounds and smeared with paint and smelling of shit and semen and oils and morning wine and she opens the door. He walks into a room away from his wife life and into the drama of women's bodies. Again. He places his hands on her breasts. Her twat. Her ass. He does not look her in the eye. His gaze is drawn elsewhere. When they embrace, and it is the embrace of carnal excess, hips ground together, chests pushing for breath, he is pulling her head back by the hair, he is turning her face to animal, he is looking at the white wall behind her. Its blankness. He presses her against it and fucks and fucks her. He sees it and sees it on the wall behind her—the image of the face. The last face he ever painted.

His ex-wife's face abstracted beyond recognition.

I love you, I did, I loved you to death.

Then he hears the performance artist snort out of her snore and murmur something and it's tonight again, and he turns to the current nymphet woman's body, which is all of their bodies, and puts his hand between her legs. Jim Morrison. Wine. A woman's body. Sex. He wakes the performance artist. Fucks her. He's himself again. Yes.

The Playwright

Night. Interior. Living room. The playwright, the poet, and the filmmaker are together in the filmmaker and writer's house. They all have a glass of scotch. It's midnight. The poet has a plan. She's laying it on them.

THE POET. Look. It's a direct action. We have to go get her.

THE FILMMAKER. Right. Let's spring her from that hell. Just what she needs. Hospitals are death houses.

THE PLAYWRIGHT. Oh my god. You're not talking about getting her out of the hospital. Are you?

THE POET. No. I'm not talking about her at all.

The playwright's circle rubbing between his thumb and forefinger seizes up, interrupted. The filmmaker jerks his head up.

THE FILMMAKER. What? Then what are we talking about?

THE POET. I'm talking about the girl.

THE FILMMAKER. What girl?

THE POET. You know what girl. The girl in the photo.

The filmmaker stands up the way a man stands up when he's thinking, Wait just a goddamn minute here.

THE FILMMAKER. Wait just a goddamn minute here. That's crazy. What are you talking about?

THE POET. I said, we're going to go get the girl. I know people. Just-this-side-of-criminal people. We can track her down. We know what town she lived in. We know what happened there, and when. And we have a photo. And we know the photographer who took the photo. I'm saying I can find her.

THE FILMMAKER. That's insane. You want to fly back to Europe and steal a human?

THE POET. Oh, I can find her.

THE FILMMAKER. Oh, really. Fine. Right. You're just going to go pluck a girl we don't know from a war zone and . . . Whatever. This is ridiculous. Okay, let's say you go all the way to Eastern Europe and you . . . you find this girl. Which is insane. What then? What the hell happens then?

THE POET. What then? We bring her here. To live with us.

The filmmaker and the playwright both start speaking at once in great incredulous waves of objections. She backs up a bit and looks at them. She crosses her arms and waits for them to peter out.

THE POET. Are you two finished? Okay, then listen. Think about it. What kind of life does this girl have there, anyway?

THE FILMMAKER. Remind me why I care? She's got nothing to do with me. With my wife. I'd rather just go get my wife.

THE POET. Listen. I know what I'm talking about. It's about the girl. Her family's atomized, she's probably living some corpse life in some pocket of hell. I mean, shit, remember how they tracked down that green-eyed Afghan girl? And she's now a *leather-faced crone*? Because her life went from misery and shit to more monotonous and meaningless misery and shit, while her famous photo went 'round and 'round the world making that McCurry guy famous? I say we do it.

THE PLAYWRIGHT. Do what, precisely?

THE POET. We do what our rising-star photographer failed to do. What all photojournalists fail to do. We go get her out of that death of a life before she dies.

THE FILMMAKER. For the love of God. *What does this have to do with my wife?*

THE PLAYWRIGHT. Whatever. This is crazy. So let's pretend it's even possible to pursue this fantasy. What does it accomplish? What is the purpose? How does it speed my sister's recovery from wherever she is?

THE POET. Listen to me. This will matter. To your wife. To your sister. I don't expect you to understand. Either of you. But you are just going to have to trust me on this. It's a . . . (*She searches the ceiling.*) It's a woman thing. If we get this girl out of her deadly circumstance and bring her here and give her a chance at a real life, it will help your wife. Your sister. The only friend I've ever given a damn about in my entire life.

THE FILMMAKER. You're serious. You are being serious?

THE POET. Look. Did you ever hear of Kevin Carter? You know, Kevin Carter. The South African photographer who took the picture of the vulture stalking a starving girl. He won a Pulitzer for that picture. Two months later he connected a hose to the exhaust pipe of his pickup truck and quietly suicided. They say he'd come back from assignments and lapse into bouts of crying, drinking, drugs. Sometimes he'd sleep for days. After he shot his prizewinning picture, they say he sat under a tree and cried and chain-smoked and couldn't get his mind away from the horror of what he saw. He checked out. People referred to him as "gone."

THE PLAYWRIGHT. Yeah. I remember. He was universally condemned for not helping the girl in the picture. He caught all kinds of shit. Said he was haunted by memories of killings, corpses, starving or wounded children, and trigger-happy madmen. So he offed himself.

THE POET. Exactly. So you get it?

The filmmaker stares at her blankly and the playwright's eye twitches.

THE POET. Don't you get it? They had a BIG argument. She said someone should have done something to get the girl out of the war zone. Your wife—*your* sister—told our friend the photographer that the prize had blood all over it. I don't think they've spoken to each other since. Didn't she tell you?

THE POET. (*Shooting for authority.*) We're going to go get that girl.

THE PLAYWRIGHT. Right. Got it. I'll finance the whole thing. The trip, the papers, whatever it takes.

THE POET. We can go to Prague first. Then on to St. Petersburg. That'll be the easy part. I know a counterfeiter in Berlin. And I know who else we'll need to get from there to Vilnius—I have people—

THE FILMMAKER. Hold on. Stop. Just . . . WAIT. What the . . . HELL are you talking about? What "people"? This isn't real. The picture. The story. The girl. None of this is real. Except . . . except that my wife is trapped in some hazed-out dreamland in a hospital and I want her back. And if I don't *do* something, I'm going to lose my mind.

A phone rings offstage. The filmmaker reluctantly goes to the kitchen and answers. His voice sounds low and muffled, almost as if he is underwater. When he returns to the living room, the blood has drained from his face.

THE PLAYWRIGHT. What? What is it? Is she all right?

THE FILMMAKER. Barely.

The three figures—filmmaker, poet, playwright—stand together for a long minute, staring at the floor. The light in the living room brightens, until they look hot and lit. The three of them look at one another.

THE FILMMAKER. You're not going to finance the whole thing. I can't let you do that.

THE PLAYWRIGHT. It's not a problem. You know I can handle it . . .

THE FILMMAKER. No, you don't understand. I have something— (*Exits stage left.*)

Sounds of a man thundering downstairs. The poet and the playwright hang in the air like inverted commas, waiting for the filmmaker. They hear pounding and something like destruction sounds, like he's down there killing something. Then they hear him coming back up the stairs in some kind of alpha-man overdrive. When he finally reappears in the living room, it's not a man's body at all. It's a giant canvas, eight feet by eight feet. Once their eyes adjust, they see that it is a painting of a giant abstract face. They hear a voice behind it as if the painting is speaking.

THE FILMMAKER. This is his painting. She kept it. Wouldn't let me burn it. I hear these things are going for over ten grand these days. (*To the playwright.*) You take it to New York. You sell it. You use the money. You do it. You get this thing out of my house.

The playwright looks up from his laptop, closes the lid. He drums with his fingers. He is seated on a blue velvet chair in an auditorium. Men and women raise little Ping-Pong paddles in the air. The auctioneer has been mouthing bids—for how long? months? years?—but the playwright has been working away silently all the while. He is interested in only one lot, only one artwork, the one he came there to sell.

Then the voice of the auctioneer arrests his attention. With his little flip of silver hair, he announces the lot: "*Facetious.* We open at ten thousand dollars. The opening bid is ten thousand dollars." The playwright snaps his head up and bites the inside of his cheek three times so he can lift his numbered little paddle. "Excellent. I have fourteen thousand dollars. The bid stands at fourteen thousand from the gentleman from New York. Do I have a—fourteen thousand, eight hundred dollars. I have fourteen thousand eight hundred. Do I have a best? Fourteen thousand eight hundred on the floor. Do we have movement? Excellent. Fifteen thousand. I have fifteen thousand dollars. We are standing at fifteen thousand from the gentleman from Lyon. Fifteen thousand, I have fifteen thousand dollars. We are at fifteen thousand. Fifteen thousand once. Fifteen thousand twice. All right, then, for the third and final time, fifteen thousand.

"And it is SOLD to the good gentleman from Lyon at fifteen thousand dollars. Very well."

The playwright looks down at the play in his laptop, and then up at the sold painting, the one he came there to sell, the one the filmmaker made him bring: a giant abstract cum-stained bloodstained face.

The Art of Identity

The performance artist's ears go full-blown tinnitus because it's the poet going Just calm down and then the playwright going Use your imagination and the filmmaker going Just wait Just wait It's not as bad as it sounds so she *amplifies* her voice and launches it at them. "It's not as bad as it sounds? You want me to fake being hollow headed all the way to Europe and *it's not as bad as it sounds*?" She can't believe it, can't believe what they are saying. This is the plan? She stares at them all like they want to eat her, saying, "You want me to do fucking *what*?"

And then it's the playwright going Look do you want me to say it all again and everyone getting impatient with her like she's a child, look at all their smug fuck faces with their *we're all a decade older than you* paternalism and her going, "Um, actually, yeah, I fucking want you to say it again because this sounds, you know, *insane*."

She crack-twists another tiny bottle of vodka open, pours it into her plastic airplane cup, slams it, then returns the empty miniature to the poet's tray table. Well, she's got to hand it to them, they fucking got her on this goddamn plane with the Nazi poet, didn't they, and they used the oldest trick in the book, the trick of Catholics and Jews. Mega-guilt. Pure and simple. When she had resisted, the poet had walked up to her and like gotten all up in her face, going Look this is the *least* you can do you're screwing him and we all know it you have been for years, you owe her this, she went, like there's some kind of woman sexual history rule book. Some kind of woman sexual sin plus-and-minus column. Like they're all holier than her. She reaches up and hits the flight-attendant-get-the-hell-over-here-I-need-a-drink button, then looks briefly at the poet, at the side of her face, and yes, she has to admit it, she's a little afraid of her.

She rubs the letter she's carrying pinned by her bra against her skin underneath her clothes. A letter from the painter. Well, you make your bed, you lie in it, that's what her mother used to say, so here she is on a plane to Eastern Europe drinking midget vodkas with a lesbian dominatrix. When the flight attendant arrives, she leans over in the flight-attendant way and says to the poet in pity hush tones, "What does she need?" Because when you're wearing a special helmet acting like you haven't enough brains to buckle a seat belt you can't be seen drinking vodka like a normal adult woman. She has a cuss-fest inside her head. The poet stamps down on her toe underneath the tray tables. She tries to make her face go slack. The poet asks the flight attendant for a pillow for her, and more vodka for herself. When the flight attendant leaves, the poet elbows the performance artist so sharply she cries out.

"What? I was just adding a little Tourette's to the scene."

When more vodka comes, the performance artist turns her head to the airplane window as far as she can. How did she get here, I mean how did she *really* get here, what were the choices, what's a past—she takes a long drink—what is *psychological development*? Is it as fucking Freudian as it sounds? She sighs the *big* sigh of twenty-six, wondering if we are all trapped inside identity, genetics, and narrative—some whacked-out Kafka god handwriting our unbearable little life stories. Then she thinks an American-artist thought, the rough-and-tumble kind: how can I use this? She rubs the letter underneath her shirt, she thinks she sees the reflection of herself in the airplane window, like a black twin, and she's falling back to memory, she prays to the god of Diamanda Galás.

Fuck.

Fuck.

Fuck.

Well, let's have it then.

When she was seven years old, a mediastinal cystic parathyroid grew in her head. The tumor, the medical professionals told her so-called parents (one a famous architect, the other a famous concert pianist, both mega-narcissists), was "inoperable." And there was this: the tumor was pushing on the beautiful gray folds of her brain in just the right way as to make her behavior look, well, there's no other way to say this . . . retarded. Like in immediate need of a helmet.

The effect this had on her mother was momentarily devastating. But that isn't the story. What her mother did with her devastation was to jettison it, and jettison it the way intellectual mega-famous narcissistic people do, until it was so buried in the layers of her psyche and her body and her motherhood that it rested at the base of her spinal cord near her fucking tailbone. She didn't shit right for years.

And what her mother—her famous concert pianist mother—did next was . . . well, a performance worthy of an ovation. Brava.

Her mother used the notoriety and fame she had garnered as a pianist to be something even bigger, better: She became a triple-A martyr, a mother of tragedy and pain, and—most important—a spokesperson. She headed every lost cause, she was awarded community prizes, was featured on *Good Morning America*. No mother in the country could outperform her, at least when it came to volunteering for lost causes, illnesses, and deformities. Cancer, AIDS, MS, cerebral palsy, Parkinson's, lupus, leprosy (yes, there is still leprosy), and all this WAY before she went third world. You get the picture.

Total abandonment of her daughter to the hired caregivers and medical staff and physical, speech, emotional, and spiritual counselors in favor of the martyr limelight.

What her father did with his devastation was a great bit more concrete; perhaps the simplest things we think about gender are utterly true.

It was his role to take the impaired daughter on excursions, so that her seemingly retarded little life didn't suck outrageously, but only mildly.

So he took her all kinds of places, even though it made his heart have a hole in it.

He took her to the movies.

He took her to McDonald's.

He took her to libraries.

He took her to the big red bull's-eye of Target.

He took her to Shari's.

He took her to water parks.

He took her to boatyards.

He took her to the beach.

He took her to bookstores.

He took her hiking in the forest.

He took her to museums.

He took her on the light rail system.

Again.

Again.

He took her horseback riding.

He took her go-cart racing.

He took her on Ferris wheels.

He took her to record stores.

He took her to music concerts.

He took her to buildings he'd designed, walking her through light and shadow and form.

He.

He.

He was more tired than any man alive, since she expressed her outrageously embarrassing glee at every one of these places he took her, all of it while wearing a helmet, and everyone always stared and said things under their breath, I mean everyone, I mean always, and at some point, no matter where they were or how it was playing out, she'd get to some frenetic moment where she was in danger of injuring herself or others, a tiny amount of drool sliding from her mouth, pee darkening the front of her crotch, the look of . . . Well, I think you can picture her grimace-smiley too-white face, right?

And so it was that one day, inside his role, this particular thing happened. She was in one of those inflatable worlds that appear at county fairs . . . the kind of inflatable hut kids can crawl inside and jump up and down. You know what I mean.

She entered.

He left.

No, really.

He left.

He left his daughter, he left his wife, his family, his life, radically and without hesitation.

Not that much later—four years, to be precise—her mother was giving a lecture on the child-tragedy circuit. Afterward, a neurosurgeon came up to her and said he knew a doctor in Europe who specialized in the type of operation they'd been told was impossible, and so nearly by accident she got her daughter a different medical team and a world-famous surgeon in Europe, and guess what?

They operated successfully and her so-called retardation disappeared and she bloomed into a completely normal, beautiful, American teen.

Completely normal, except for the pearly skull scar and the emotional scars for fucking life.

And *that's* how she comes to be sitting in an airplane with the poet pretending to be her past. Because she's a stand-in. She's a retarded girl again, being taken to Europe for experimental treatment again, a story from her real past invading her present. Because without makeup and face jewelry and vintage clothes and hair products, without anything on her head besides that disgusting helmet, she looks much younger than she is. Just past puberty. Which means they can swap her. Which means they can use her special retard-girl identity papers to enter the country with her, but leave the country with a different girl. Later, someone will come back and get her and take her back home.

It's the *least* she can do.

And besides, the poet had said, this is the most radical performance art she'll ever do in her life.

Emotional cripple. Adult need machine. Fuck addict. American artist. She rubs the scar on her head. She rubs the letter against her flesh. The last thought she thinks before she drops into a twenty-something-year-old vodka sleep is: I hate women.

The House of Art

For more than a year, the girl and the widow live together in the widow's house while her childhood shifts. When the girl arrives she is eleven. When the girl leaves she is nearly thirteen.

Inside, the widow starts to teach the girl everything she knows about art. The history of photography, painting, music, literature. "Look at this poem. How it travels down the page in lines, not sentences. How its beauty is vertical, like a body." The girl puts her fingers on the page, against the words, tracing their meanings, touching them and touching them. Silently mouthing.

The widow shows her poetry and science, philosophy and myths from all over the world. She teaches her how religion and science each rely on a violent faith between creation and destruction. She shows her how the history of art carries with it the same duality. She shows her the body—Christ's body endlessly crucified, bodies in war and sacrifice, the never-ending bodies of women, bodies in pleasure or pain or sleep or death, bodies in rapture, tortured bodies, bodies in prayer, bodies in the static pose of a portrait. The widow tells the girl, "Do not listen to what any society tells you about the body—the body is the metaphor for all experience. A woman's body more than any other. Like language, its beautiful but weaker sister. Look at this poem. This painting. Look at these photographs. The body doesn't lie."

The widow weaves the importance of expression and representation into the smallest details of an ordinary life. She milks the goat and steals the chickens' eggs while telling stories of archetypal animals. She lights the fire and cleans the dishes while reciting poetry of love or war. She walks miles to the nearest village and brings back underground writings and photos, the same as milk and bread and sugar and coffee and ink and paper, making sure to detail the seriousness of these suppressed objects. She is careful to explain to the girl how it is that human expression is the highest value in life, but so too is death, in this place and time they find themselves inhabiting. The girl takes in everything, rarely speaking, her listening and watching a kind of devouring.

One day the girl is taking a bath and calls out. The widow comes into the tiny bathroom and the water surrounding the girl's legs is clouded with crimson. She slaps the girl in the face and smiles and kisses her on the cheeks. She says, "May you bloom." The girl doesn't flinch. The widow tells her, "This is the first language of your body. It is the word *ne*. When you bleed each month, as when the moon comes and goes in its journey, you leave the world of men. You enter the body of all women, who are connected to all of nature." The girl asks, "Why is it the word *ne*?" The widow responds, "When you bleed, this word is more powerful than any word you could ever speak. It is a blood word. It binds you to animals and trees and the moon and the sun. Where men take blood in the world in hunting and war, women give blood. It is the word *ne* because it closes the room of a woman's body to men." The widow places her hands into the water and says, "Good. You are alive. You and I are alive."

The girl's mind floats.

This is not her first bleeding.

Her first bleeding came at age seven, after her fourth rape, four years before her family exploded before her eyes. She had been buying paper. Her mother was across the street at the post. She could still see her mother even as her own body was yanked by a soldier and dragged behind a wall. Her mother searched and searched, nearly losing her mind, until a soldier marched her mother out of town at gunpoint. Having been left for dead in an alley, she lay there for an entire day, into dusk's falling, thinking, Death is a gift sometimes. Almost sacred. Like a door to something beautiful and profound.

But she did not die. And so it was that on that day, shivering in the alley, her hand moved instinctively to her rose of being and there was blood. Of course there was blood; but this blood was not the blood of soldiers' forced entrances, dried and day old and smelling of what goes wrong in men. Triggered early, this blood moved through her like a warm river. New and wet and dark and smelling lightly of metal. Reminding her of steel traps. Of animals. In this way, when what she probably needed was warmth, food, water, and more than anything else in the world, the tenderness of a woman, the quiet hush and caress of her mother, she reached down and found only her own small being, red and hot. She brought her hand up to look at it. She tasted it. Salt and copper. Slippery like oil between her fingers.

Her first thought: I want to paint.

So she dragged her body back to the barn next to her own house even as she could barely walk or stand or bear the weight of anything and she found a wooden plank and she took what was left of her strength and painted with her own menstrual blood. That is how her parents and brother found her. Almost like a wild animal.

As she looks at the red water around her now in the bath, the girl thinks, That is the blood that has returned to me now. The blood I have waited for. And she thinks of the wolf's paw, the severing she witnessed one night when she first came to this house.

The widow shows the girl how to use a pad to carry the blood close to her body, and in the months to come the girl's and the widow's monthly bleedings synchronize. From that day forward, the widow accelerates her teachings. She teaches the girl how to be present in her skin, how to leave it; how to kill animals to eat them and to use their skins and fur; how to extract medicine from drying and grinding their internal organs; how to chop wood; dig your way to food or shelter; how to shoot to hunt, how to shoot to kill a man; how to use your hands to make things. How to hold charcoal to draw, how to make oil paints, what a sable brush is; how to take a pinhole photo using a box and the sun; how to hold a violin and draw a bow against its thin, unimaginable strings; how to make language go strange and vertical to make a poem. How to trust the moon.

Sometimes, when the widow is retrieving more wood for the fire, or when she is gathering materials to close a hole in the wall or roof, or when she is milking the goat or digging up frozen potatoes or shooting fowl or retrieving a rabbit from a trap, the woman catches a glimpse of the girl in the act of painting. Out in the barn. On scraps of wood. With colors she has invented from berries and roots and olive oil and mud. She paints with her bare hands. And sometimes, the widow sees her paint with her own blood, her hand dipping down to the well of her body. When she watches the girl paint with blood, it takes her breath straight out of her, lifting it up to a place she has not admitted to for years. Frenzied and animal the girl's hands are. Wild, her blond tangles of hair. Her body thrusting forward and retreating with an unbashful sexuality. Without anyone's permission or knowledge. Sometimes the girl is laughing. Sometimes she shouts, "*Ne*!"

What she paints: a face. And the face is either screaming or laughing, at what it is impossible to tell.

The woman then understands that the girl will someday leave the house. Maybe soon. That the force within this girl is not anything belonging to the widow. And because she sees something that the girl does not, the woman starts to teach her English. She tells her, "Someday you must leave here and take what we have left in us to America. What we have left in us, buried and ravaged as it is, needs to come out. It is not a perfect place, America. It's simply a way out of this story."

In this way art becomes the whole world of the girl. And her hands become painter's hands; and her body leans toward becoming; and her tongue begins to move from the cornered shapes of one language into the rounded edges of another; her dreams begin to carry scenes from an unknown country; and her origins, which are a white blast zone, begin to seek form, like the crouch of violence in her fingers, like the unstoppable sex of a child leaving childhood, making for the world.

Part Three

o o o o

Love Is an Image

It's quiet like snow.

The filmmaker is holding the writer's hand in the hospital room.

His head is on the bed near her chest.

Their breathing—a husband's, a wife's—synchronizes and hums with the hospital's life-machine sounds.

Their beautiful boy is walking around the room with his Canon camcorder. Filming the lines on the linoleum floor, the fluorescent lights of the ceiling, the IV going from its transparent bag of liquid down the thin tube to his mother's arm, the TV with his mother's heartbeat signals, the somber hang of the curtains. Filming himself in the little mirror above the sink. He turns to the bed. His father and mother look asleep. He walks as quietly as he can toward their faces. With his six-year-old finger he pushes the zoom until the faces fill the frame, then farther, until it's just his mother, then just his mother's eye and cheek and hair . . . everything.

Where White Is

I am into a white. As white as snow covering a field, stretching out toward all horizons. As white as a page. If there is a surrounding forest or mountain or city I cannot see them beyond the white.

I don't know how long I've been here, or how deeply in I have traveled. I am aware that outside this place there is a room, and in the room they say a woman is not well. I think the woman is me, but I am so far away I cannot breathe language back into her, and so she rests, like a sleeping body, like a sentence yet unformed.

Sometimes I can feel my husband's body—his physical presence—in my bones, and so I know when he has entered the room. He cannot enter the white. And sometimes I can smell my son's breath and hair and skin, and I want to rip my heart from my chest and hurl it.

To them, I must look dead.

But I am not dead.

The white is soft. Soft against the eyes and the body, soft in your ears and throat. Not like mist or smoke. As if the air around you suddenly had dimension. You can almost touch it. This white before you. Where I am.

Inside the white I can hear things and see things. Sounds and images resolve and dissolve at random intervals. And different times present themselves—different times from my life or the lives of people I've known or the lives of random people, little scenes of being, all of them come and go.

The stories here move differently from the way they do out there. Inside the white, stories move backward and forward in time and appear in all places at once. Language and images split into thousands of universes. Stories and people and images connect with faster-than-light transfers of information. Many worlds coexist.

I do not feel unconscious or crazy or comatose. I feel part of the motion of all matter and energy, and thus I am a participant with agency. If I want something to come or go, it does.

I hear something now inside the white. It is a word. The name of a street: Bakszta.

The name of the street is immediately comforting. It is the street of my ancestors. The only one in the world who knows the people who lived there and their names, names that became my name, the name that began as one word and deteriorated down and down and under and across until it was utterly atomized into my American last name, the only one left: *me*. Because of all the daughters, some of them childless, I am the last. I am a locus.

Juknevicius. A name.

Bakszta. A street.

Through the white: a girl.

It is her. The girl who haunts me.

I go through the possibilities again. Maybe she is my dead daughter. And maybe she is me, or some relative before me. Maybe the girl is simply a metaphor for what we lose or what we make. And maybe the girl is just a girl, an imagined one, one created from the mind of a woman lost in the spaces between things.

I open my mouth to speak.

Perhaps it is the name of the street.

Perhaps it is the name of the girl.

Perhaps it is the name of my son, or my husband.

Or just a name, my name, my brother's, a friend's, an artist's, a poem, a country, any name.

But no name comes from my mouth.

My voice—language—is swallowed up by the white.

I see the girl's blond tangled hair as she walks away from me into the white, into some other story. I hear a blasting sound. I follow her.

The white turns to a scene of war. Like a movie.

I open a door in a bar in an Eastern European village. My husband and son are there too, but I am not near them. I am near other people—artists who are dear to me. My brother. The poet, the photographer, all of them. I can see my husband and my son, though. Across the space. They've made hats from paper cups. They are laughing. My husband is drinking beer. My son is drinking apple cider. His cheeks little apples. Someone is playing a guitar. Someone else is playing an accordion. There is amber-colored wood on the floors and walls and chairs. People seem intimately close, like in a not-American bar. Their faces warm and rosed. Their gestures swept up in song or laughter. No one is picking up on anyone, or arguing, or using money, or wearing a certain thing. No one's hair matters. This is a not-American room, a room not made for money and action and ready-made lust thrusts, a room where people are speaking intellectually while drunk, the artists and the farmers giving each other equal weight, and leaning into one another's bodies without concern—men leaning into men's bodies and women into women's—so that the air of it carries all of our hearts and loosens all of our minds and anyone could be from any country for this moment. Loving anyone they want. Saying anything.

The myriad conversations make a kind of voice-hum over the room, and I look up at my husband and my son and I smile.

But there is a war raging just outside, and the information comes to be known that we are all about to die, that a thermonuclear blast is coming. The information is coarse and immediate, as I assume it is for farm animals. They catch the smell, their spine fur shivers, they shift weight from one leg to another, feel restless, look up. The time we have left is understood. I hear it and know it and within ten seconds I make my way to the beating heart of love (my husband and son) so that we can be inside a group embrace, looking into the planets of one another's eyes as the white life-ending cataclysm occurs.

The embrace and the blast happen at once, comfort and annihilation. Our bodies the universe.

I am in the white again.

Energy never dying.

Just changing forms.

I lie down in the white.

I know why I am here.

I've come to ask my questions. The ones my dead girl left inside me.

Is it my fault.

What happened to you.

Are you happy.

What do you want from me.

The girl is here, inside the white. When the time is right, I will ask her my questions. And then I will either go back or she will take me.

The woman in the room, the one who is maybe me, they say she is dying in a hospital bed.

Bloodsong

The widow is in the kitchen making soapy circles with her hands on plates at the sink. I can hear her humming. How long have I lived here with her? How old am I? Am I still a girl?

I am looking at the widow's book of paintings of the crucifixion of Christ. It is beautiful, this book of Christ paintings. It is the size of my entire torso. Death, I've learned, she lives in all of us the moment we are born. The pink wrinkled skin of a squirming infant can't hide it. It's just true. Maybe that is why there are almost no paintings of babies—except the Christ child, and what kind of baby is that? A fat little fiction—a baby that comes from the sky through the body of a dim-witted woman.

All bodies are death bodies. But the best death body of all is the crucifixion. A beautiful womanman hanging naked from a cross, stuck with nails, bleeding, thorn headed. Of all of them, I love the Velázquez the most. I am looking at it now. I lower my head to the image and close my eyes and rest my cheek upon his body. I put my mouth to the page and lick it. I wish it was in me.

I can feel my body. I can feel the heat at my chest and ribs and belly. I follow the heat story with my hand. I can make fire between my legs any time I like. I open my eyes and raise my head from the page of the Christ body. I look at it. I don't care about this puny faith. I have died and been resurrected hundreds of times. What's the Christ story compared to the bloodsong of one girl? How flimsy that story is. I believe in Velázquez. With our hands and art. I believe we must make the stories of ourselves.

My name is Menas. This is my story.

There was a bomb.

Once I asked the widow, when I could not find the story in any of her carefully collected news accounts: where is the story of my bomb? There is no war, she told me. There's been no war for fifty years. There is only the occupation, and what that has meant to people. Your family killed. My husband sent to Siberia. The bomb that killed your family? . . . Listen to me. No one knows where it came from.

What has happened to us—there is no story.

But there was a family. My father the poet. My mother the weaver. My brother, my other, child gone to ash. I am like a blast particle—a piece of matter that was not destroyed, a piece of something looking for form.

There is the widow and her house and how I came here. Through the violence of men, through the forest, across a snow-covered field. I do not believe in the word *meilė*—love. Nor *tëvynei*—love for one's country. Nor *vaikams*—love for children. *Motinos*—maternal love. None of them. In the place of love there is art.

There is my body and what has happened to it.

There is painting.

I paint on wood. Sometimes the widow and I pull the sides of abandoned houses apart. My paintings are of girls. In one painting a girl is chewing off her own arm, her hand caught in a steel trap. In another, a girl's mouth has a house in it. Unlike a photograph, my girl faces are blurry. I want them to be blurry. I always make myself stop from putting them right, for what will it mean? Right for whom? By whose hands? The face of a girl should be blurry. Like she's running.

There is a history to art, I've learned. Religion. Philosophy. Myth. Photography. I am reading about them. But there are chapters, whole books, missing. I see the stories of women, but they are always stuck inside the stories of men. Why is that?

The widow fills a kettle and puts it on the stove.

I pull down from the shelves a book of world mythology and my sadness grows. Artemis, why the paler sister of Apollo, whom she brought through blood into the world from her mother's womb with her own hands? I turn to the section about my part of the world, and in the mythology of my so-called people—the goddesses—what use are they? Why did I ever like these stories? What is Gabija, goddess of fire, who protects against unclean people? I do not need this protection. It is a trick to place fear there. What use is Laima, goddess of fate, luck, childbirth, marriage, and death, if she keeps women inside the house, away from the open space of the world? Saulė—saint of orphans, symbol of the sun . . . who cannot teach me what the fire inside me is. Who would have me put it out, or give it to a man? Still, I have torn pictures of them all from books and pasted them next to my own paintings in the barn, hoping for company. Though I find it hard to trust them. I wonder about what they want.

The kettle sings. The widow pours hot water into a cup filled with tea leaves.

History, mythology, literature, all the pictures and stories in time: women as witches and monsters, women as prizes and slaves, women as frozen bodies. A woman burning on a stick, queens about to lose their heads. Where are the artists? Where are the bodies who would break out of the story and rescue the others? Where are the daughters with fire in them?

I reach for another book: Indian mythology. It's easy to find the page I want. I have looked at it so many times I can smell my skin on it. It is a painting of Kali. Great mother. Killer. Next to her image, her story.

Once upon a time, there was a war. A young woman named Durga was facing a demon named Raktabija. Durga wounded the demon, in lots of ways and with many weapons, but she made things worse, because for every drop of blood that was spilt, the demon made a copy of himself. The battlefield was filled with him. Durga, in need of help, prayed for Kali to fight the demons. With a gaping mouth and red eyes, Kali killed the demon by sucking the blood from his body and putting the many demons in her mouth. She ate them. Then she danced on the field of battle, stepping on the dead bodies.

I do not care about India, or Hinduism, or Buddhism. I do not need a savior.

It's the art of her.

I stare and stare at it. I can feel the blood under my skin. Her picture gets inside me, so that we are not two, but one. No longer a picture, but a mirror. I open my mouth. I stare at the image until it is everything, and I go, I mean I literally leave and go wherever the image takes me, and I am glad, for I have no ties to this world. Such images make me a different kind of alive. I become the thing I am looking at. Her body my body. I touch between my legs. Heat. My mouth fills with spit.

Bloodthirsty warrior mother. I envy her tongue and might. Can this house even hold the two us?

The widow drinks tea and reads from an underground newspaper; she says Democracy is coming.

An Invisible Union

I've never written about this. I've not told anyone. To my knowledge, the experience exists only in memory between us, a writer and a photographer, but it has no representation, so it may not even be real.

The camera had nothing to do with anything. It didn't matter.

I'm lying. It did matter. It mattered that she used a camera. It mattered so much that my mouth fills with spit as I think of her, even now.

For example. She walked into the white room of our motel. She stripped the mattress white.

This is important. The whiteness. And her volition.

She was dressed in tight black pants, tight black sleeveless cotton shirt, Gap-like and stiff and new. Her hair the precise wheat color of mine, only short and raging. Her eyes the precise transparent blue of mine, but more driven. Us both Geminis but not quite twinning. Sexual questions between us—her insistently straight, me bisexual—the what of it.

Her camera gave her self-possession. I did not expect her to direct things; I thought she would want me to. But immediately she said lie down on the mattress. I did it. Her voice was calm and quiet. She said take off your pants. I did it. She said take off your shirt. I did it. Sweat formed on my upper lip simply from her asking me to do ordinary things. From language out of the mouth of a woman. She said touch yourself. I petted myself lightly. Heat. She said close your eyes. I did. I heard the first click of the camera. She said—but it was not as if she was saying it—it was the power of the camera in front of her face giving her the means to direct things—squeeze the meat of your pussy until you are wet. I did. That's when I felt her eye on me close in—the lens of her. She said take one of your tits out of your bra and squeeze it like it's full of milk. I did. She said milk it. I did. My mouth opened barely. My pussy became wet.

She said take off your panties. She said take off your bra.

I heard her steady the camera. She said whatever you do, don't open your eyes again. I don't. Everything becomes present and past tense, like in a photo.

She says play with your tits. First, I squeeze the full-palmed whole of each breast, kneading them up and out as if I am readying them to be devoured. They become swollen and my nipples harden. I pinch my own tits over and over again thinking I will make them red for her, I will make them mouthable and hard and huge and reddened. I picture them as I play with them. I keep working them until I can feel them becoming the picture I want. I can hear the camera and I can feel her moving in and out and in and out. When she is near I feel heat, and while I am pinching my tits I can't help it: I undulate my hips and my pussy begins to cream.

She says play with your tits again so I start to shake them by holding my nipples and jiggling my tits. This makes me arch and moan and I lift my hips up to where I imagine she might be. Then I cup each tit with each of my hands and jiggle it for her like a porn-paid woman might for some sap of a man. She says put your hand up yourself and I do, and my pussy becomes swollen and like a begging mouth.

I moan and whine.

I can feel her photographing me. I can hear the shutter clicks. I think I might lose my mind.

I pull my own tits up so hard it makes me cry out. I push them together and I wait and wait doing that until I cannot wait any longer and then I shove one tit up to my mouth and suck my own nipple. I bite and suck myself. I say *please* and spit covers things. I can feel her lens very close to me but not touching me and I think a little this is what it is like to go insane.

Or this is desire, convulsive.

It is no wonder men cheat.

It is no wonder women cheat.

Desire is larger than god.

Ask a believer.

While I'm sucking myself hard and wild like an animal or infant, I suddenly hear her say play with yourself.

I let go of my tits and they drop like fallen faith.

I move my hands down. She says pull yourself apart first and show me. She says show me your clit, I want to see your swollen clit. I do it. I drive my hips toward her voice. I think I hear her use a zoom. I fuck the air showing her my clit and my wide-open pussy, as slowly as possible. The throbbing seems like it's bringing me close to death.

She says finger your clit. She says play with it between your thumb and forefinger, hard. I do it. She says with your other hand shove your fingers up into yourself. I do. I think I am maybe panting and sighing or crying. My fingers are swimming. I'm creaming. She says taste yourself. I do. She says now lift your legs up show me all of yourself. Make yourself come for me.

I can't see her, but I know the camera is nearly touching me at the site of all creation.

If a camera could record smell and heat and taste.

Click. And click. Clicking like sparks.

I begin to cry inside my ecstatic state, I am close to release, she knows it, she photographs it a frame at a time, I picture the obscene position I am in, I am close to surrender without touching anyone or anything except this woman with her lens.

When I come I make an animal sound and the shiver overtakes me endlessly. The cum shoots from my body in a way that has never happened before. Like a man's. I come and I cry. The shivering lasts several minutes. This opening that is me, it opens and closes in violent contractions, the dark of the inside of me meeting the light of the white walls, the production of an image, the intimacy of art, the space between two women, everything balanced in its dark and light. My eyes still closed, I feel the weight of her body, finally. She lies on top of me, naked. That's all. She doesn't move. She asks me not to move. She cries, and her tears fall on my face, wetted whispers.

When I open my eyes she is back in a chair in the corner, sitting like a beautiful and quiet bird. Taking film from the camera. As if it was all the camera.

She never speaks to me that way again.

This is the only night between us like this.

Journey to the Underworld

After the poet has slept the sleep of crossing countries.

After she has moved through the rooms and faces, the déjà vu and pulse, the light and shadow of Prague—the mother of cities—and entered its black-and-blue night.

After she has taken the performance artist—spoiled brat—to the apartment of a Russian washed-up gymnast turned sculptor—dearest friend—who will take the young woman in for as long as it takes. An apartment shared with a post-op Czech transsexual. Overlooking the river Neva.

After she has dined with her friend the poet journalist from *Krasny 100%*. They talk the talk of outsider writers. The poet is warm in her chest.

After she has gotten drunk with the poet journalist and his friends—a collage artist and his contortionist cousin—after she has witnessed the sexual excess of all of them together in a five-star hotel room, the impossible bend and lurch of the cousin's body, her eating herself, her howl still animal in her head. How travel loosens sexuality until it hops like a parasite from host to host, feeding, always feeding.

After she has made her way into the further night of this city—walking with sex smeared against her pants and thighs, and alcohol still blurring her vision and the taste of blood, cum, and ecstasy still tangy on her tongue—this city haunted by its own past, the ever-lit-up Crystal Palace with its winding bulbs and sword spires, the opulent squares and palaces seemingly divorced from modernity, the pieces of land fondled by the finger of the Neva River, kissed by the tides of the Baltic Sea. City of waters. Canals. Rivers. Lakes. Floating city. City of a night sky reflected in waters. City of lost names: Petrograd. Leningrad. City of revolutions: Decembrist. February. October. Bolshevik. Lenin's Great Terror. Stalin's Red Purge. City of Dostoyevsky. Akhmatova. The Stray Dog Café. Pushkin. Gogol. Tchaikovsky. Shostakovich. Nabokov. City of white nights. City of the stone of tsars carved through with animals and poverty and piss-stained alleyways. City of women trafficked like fruit. City of locally grown poppies and the sweet stench of Black. City of child junkies. City of gypsies. City of porn with the thick-tongued accents of Soviet-era fantasies. City of war and sexuality. City of domination and submission.

City of the Tambov Gang.

She has not come here for the Summer Literary Seminars. Not this time.

Greshniki. The Sinners Club. A gay club styled as an old mansion taking up four floors. The motto of the club: "We're all sinners. We're all equal." So many rooms: a dance floor with mirrors, a balcony, a restaurant, a video Internet bar with free wireless access, and a "dark room." Young naked men dance all night on the stage, their flex and thick getting under the skin. Her sitting at a table.

This is where she is to meet the man from the Tambov Gang. When he walks up she is writing a poem.

I've weaved my way to stand
between two seated, manly queens
dressed down in thin denim.
The boy on stage, sexual
and sure, enters his finale.
I'm drunk. I've never felt
such love in any room.
I join the thick applause,
cry and lurch a little, ignore
a hissed sit down! sit down!
and pursed lips from the drink
I've spilled with a light hip-check,
launch more hoarse cheers,
monstrous American daughter
with real tits, tears without salt,
snotty air-whistles, a real cunt.

When the man from the Tambov Gang touches her arm, she looks up and she is startled by his exquisite androgyny. It takes her American breath away.

"You will drink, then?" His voice a masterpiece of Slavic history.

"Yes," she offers, letting her hands go slack on the tabletop.

He looks to the bar, snaps his fingers, and sits.

The music's beat massages the soles of her feet, the chairs. She can feel it in her palms on the table.

"Do you have a light?" He leans toward her with a brown cigarette.

The poet commits chivalry. Pulls the silver lighter from her leather jacket pocket. Lights the cigarette. Smiles at his smile curling under the veil of smoke. He is wearing gray sleeveless mesh. His arms are . . . written. Tattooed in a language she sees as beautiful skin symbols. He looks at the stage. Laughs deeply. Then throws his beautiful head back into a deeper laugh, his blond sculpted hair like oiled wood shavings, his lips full and wet, his neck smooth and exposed. He turns back to her.

"It is good like vodka, yes? It is like holding something very good in your mouth, before you swallow, these boys . . ." He laughs again. " . . . these beautiful boys."

The poet examines the thinness of his skin. She thinks perhaps she can see the veins gleaming. The skin of Russians and Baltic peoples—so white it carries other colors. Blue. Green.

Four vodkas arrive. In shot glasses. No ice. As they do here. He says, "We drink Zyr first. It is not perfect, but it is not American either, yes?" Laughing, he drinks the shot in a single gulp, and she follows, holding the cold in her mouth, letting her teeth take it. They eat little crackers immediately. In the way of this part of the world. "Again?" They kill the next two. He laughs. He looks at her—around the whole of her, his eyes outlining. Then he says, "Next is coming the Jewel of Russia Classic . . . you will not be able to stand it." He smokes the cigarette and the music thuds up through their spines and the boys move and move and she wants more and more.

They drink four shots of the Jewel of Russia before he says, "We talk now?" But another four vodkas have arrived, and he holds his hand up with something like the power of history. "No. We drink. *This*. This is something the world did not expect." He holds his glass to hers and taps it. The sound coming from his mouth: *za ná-shoo dróo-zhboo*. He has made a toast. They drink.

In the poet's mouth the vodka becomes a poem: a slight oiliness. A hint of apple. Faintly sweet. And the burn. Pleasing. She closes her eyes and lingers there. She opens her eyes and mouth and says, "What is this?"

"Chopin. Isn't that simple? Distilled from potatoes, of course. Stubborn Poles. But what they have done to us all! The irony." And his laugh fills the space around them like a cave swallowing a body whole.

"Now. We talk. Yes?"

"Yes." The word emerging from her lips like something she can taste.

He puts his cigarette in an ashtray, crosses his arms over his chest and leans back a bit in his chair, lifting his chin up, looking down on her, but not with malice. "I have a question for you. Why do you seek this girl? This girl is unknown to you, yes? Is it a little pet that you want? Or will she be . . . a commodity, perhaps?" He smiles, barely.

"Nothing like that. We just want to get her out. I can't explain." The words sound impotent even to her.

"I see. Just another American taking the world's children from harm to safety. What a wondrous benevolence. Just like your American movie stars, yes? The power of American . . . love." He picks the cigarette back up, takes a graceful drag, and blows a smoke ring upward. She stares at its slow, blue ascension. "And money!" His laugh thunderous. "You know, you do not look what I expected."

"No? How so?" She curls around his words, cautious as prey.

"You do not look as . . . commanding as I hear you are."

She feels him study the face of her, the neck, the collarbone, her hands.

"But then, this is a facet to your personality behind closed doors, is it not?" Again he throws his head back, laughing deep enough to drug someone unconscious.

She wonders briefly how he knows this. Then decides it is part of his job to know, and anyway, it is mind-bogglingly flattering. Think of it: a worldwide reputation. The admiration of this lyric-mouthed Russian androgyne gangster. She wishes he would look through her hard enough to slice her open.

The wickedly beautiful man from the Tambov Gang then puts his glass down hard on the table. He looks at her seriously. "I make you this deal. I give you the papers you need. The passport. The transport instructions. Who will be your help. And then," he leans in like a thief, "we go then. You and I. From here, tonight. I want that you will help me with something. I want to put the power into your"—he covers her hand with his— "capable American hands."

There is no good reason to agree to this. In anyone else's life it would signal danger. Maybe even death. But this is not anyone else's life, and she has lived hers on the edges of things . . . and what is a life if one cannot walk into the night with a stranger? Following the universal instincts of leather life, then, she turns her palm up underneath his hand until it is nearly a handshake and says, "For you, then?"

"No. Alas, not for me, beautiful hard woman." He stares at her. His eyes echo the waterways of this city, centuries haunting the pupils. "For someone I know who has suffered enough that he cannot feel his own skin. Do you know this kind of suffering?"

The poet nods her head. Suffering happens in all places, doesn't it, all times, in the flesh of any skin, in the hollow of what should be a heart.

"His family, killed. Like so many . . . Bosnian. But choose your country these days. No?"

The poet nods again.

"There is only one cure for this suffering. Violence for violence. I think you can help him to feel his skin again. Even for one night only. For me you can do this?"

The poet nods.

"Good." He puts his hand on her shoulder. They both look

at the boy body on stage, its cock and hips, its torso, its incomprehensible physical truth. Then he turns to her and slaps her cheek—the blood rushing to the surface of her skin—"But the money too, of course!"

The poet nods.

The Violence of Language

The performance artist sits, motionless, in the empty kitchen of a Russian and a Czech who are strangers to her. Deposited here by the poet to help save the life of the writer. In a city that holds no meaning for her. Looking out the window at an overcast sky, heavy with almost-rain. A very old stone bridge. Water. Birds. Lamps. An emptied-out self. She's tired. She doesn't know these people, this city. She's drinking vodka in the morning from a small antique shot glass.

Somehow the burden of it—handing over her identity, agreeing to wait a month to be taken home—somehow, though it depresses her mind, it thrills her flesh. As if her body knows something she does not. She hates the flesh thrill, resents it, and yet she cannot not feel it. Like a fire just getting born. Something she carries against her chest like a beating heart. Letting her know she is alive.

The performance artist pulls the letter from the painter out from beneath her shirt. She has kept it there, in her bra against her tit, for three days. Day and night. Her skin smell on the envelope comforts her. At least she has this. This letter from the painter. Strange lifeline in this insane story they've abandoned her inside. On purpose she has not opened it. Especially not in front of the poet. On purpose she has guarded its contents like intimacy itself. For she loves him. She loves him more than her own life. She loves this man they have ejected from their fucking reality, so much that she almost can't breathe thinking about him. In her heart and beyond she knows she is the only one who truly knows him. The only one willing to go all the way with him. Through the crucible of sex and art. Through the excess of him. Through the story of all their tangled-up lives, down into the hell of him, like Persephone. The man who nearly murdered his wife. The unapologetic alcoholic artist. A love unto death, if necessary. And he will fucking love this. That she did this thing. He will see that she is like him. And when this all ends, well, she'll go wherever with him. No one will be able to stop her. And the two of them will make art and make love and leave the world of the rest of them. She drinks, and drinks, until things liquefy.

She brings the letter to her face, closes her eyes, and smells it. She can see his face, feel his body. Something like sapphires under her tongue. She slips a finger underneath where he has licked the paper with his own spit. She opens the envelope. She pulls the paper—thin white—from the envelope, her heart beating, beating:

Well, here it is.

I am leaving you.

By the time you read this, I'll be in Paris in the arms of another woman. One I've known for years. One of many. This thing between us, it wasn't anything. And now it's gone sour, too complicated. I'll have none of it. You are too close to the black hole of my past.

You know I am no good with words, so this will be abbreviated, but true. Or true enough. Fuck words anyway.

I'm giving you something though. A diptych of a life.

I will not be seeing you again. I've cleared all trace of you from my loft, and when I return, if you come here, I won't let you in. Don't try. I will never visit your loft again either. If I see you in the street, I won't acknowledge you. You no longer exist. But I am giving you something. For your art. Try to remember that.

This will hurt.

1.

The year before I shot her, there was a night when we had an argument. One in a series. We were both skunk-ass drunk. At one point she grabbed a knife and ran into the bathroom—locked herself in there. I threw my weight against the door but nothing happened. I laughed. Then I slumped down on the floor against the door and fell asleep. When she opened the door, the first thing I saw was her blond bush—eye level. Then she thrust out her fucking arm and I saw my name, with blood like a dot-to-dot, carved into her arm. She immediately went back into the hole of the bathroom. I walked to the kitchen, grabbed a serrated bread knife, and hacked her name into my own arm in stick-man strokes. I still have the scar of her. The word of her. On my arm. In certain light.

2.
A year later, one night, I was deep into my drunk in the living room. It was peaceful. I was naked. She was in the bedroom asleep. I'd picked up a gun earlier in the day from a junkie I knew. A 9mm Beretta. I had the gun resting on my thigh, near my dick. I'd had it that way for hours. I heard her stir. She came into the living room. She was naked. The years of . . . what is it? Passion? Chaos? Death? In the air between us. I don't know why. I pointed the gun at the wife of her. She lifted her hand up. I shot. I hit her hand and her shoulder. In the dark, she dropped to the floor like a beautiful felled black-and-blue goose. We didn't move like that, the smell of the shot hanging in the air, for long minutes. Love is a gun.

There. Don't say I never gave you anything.

Perhaps you can make your performance of this man and this woman into something. Art is everything.

You know, every street in Paris is wet. Every person in Paris has a dog. Every hand in Paris holds a cigarette. Every mouth in Paris is a kiss.

Last night I dreamt myself covered in paint; the paint may have been blood. It was warm, like a bath almost. It seemed to look good on my skin. Beauty. Death. The same. Drink yourself drowned. Cut your skin with knives. Fuck with your genitals. Paint a painting. Shoot a gun. American.

I tell you, it scares me what I have done to her.

It terrifies me, even.

And yet I am not sorry.

I am as deeply unsorry as a person could be.

There is nothing that one human will not do to another.

Ce n'est pas rien. Au revoir.

The performance artist. Her idea of herself . . . drifts weightless as an astronaut in her skull. Her chest hollows. Her body goes slowly numb. Her hair. Her face. Her hands. Nothing. The air she is breathing. Useless. Thoughtless.

She folds the letter back up and places it again against her skin. She pats it against her chest as if she is much older. She looks out of the window, but sight . . . sight just isn't in her right now. She stands up. Puts a coat on. In a regular way. Thinking, it isn't necessary. Just be molecules. Light. She gently wraps her neck in a blue wool scarf hanging next to the door—someone's. She opens the door to the flat. Steps out. Closes it. She walks down the hallway. Down several flights of stairs, her feet on the steps not connected to anything.

She opens the big wooden door to the stage of outside. St. Petersburg. She steps out onto the walkway. Just be light. She stops, closes her eyes, takes in a big breath . . . blows it out slowly, like tiny white moths from her mouth. Like all the body's memories leaving as light. In her head: a man leaves.

She walks to the bridge.

Stands dead center.

History makes the distance from the bridge to the water epic, dramatic, artful.

She places her hands on the historic stone. She looks down at the water, a kind of gray that is nearly black, washing sins away. City smells float around her. Pedestrians are perfectly absent. It begins to rain, lightly. Her age makes her look like a painting. The girl in pain or love. She leans over the ledge of things, her stomach and chest pressed hard against the stone. She can see the pink-and-white flesh of her hands. The blue of the wool scarf. She can hear the water so precisely it is like voices. Why, when she was a child, didn't anyone teach her to swim? But she knows why. She was the imperfect child. Dumbed and drooling. Love lost to her from the get-go. She does not know where her father ever went. Her mother lost to philanthropy and activism in a celebrity world. The stone underneath her is as hard as anything in the world. Her ribs under her clothes no longer feel necessary. She lets the air leave her lungs. Molecules. Light. All the world's a stage. We are all of us without origin. Who's to say we were ever here at all? She closes her eyes. She can feel the letter against her chest, near her breast, where her heart should be. And then she pushes forward. The toppling body of a young woman with nowhere left to perform love.

Sometimes it takes so little to make an ending.

Triptych

1.

Gunfire in the distance. The photographer is washing her face in the tiny bathroom of another random family's home in Eastern Europe. Even as she's been gone for more than a year, somehow the poet has found her, and wants to meet with her, about the girl in the photo. She doesn't want to. She dries her face and looks in the mirror and sees the woman she was and the woman she is, at war with each other. She moves back into the family. All the motion and energy in the house moves toward dinner. None of them looks up, and she is glad to be this unnoticed. She wishes she could lose her identity altogether. Potatoes go into a pot. A mother's roughened hands. Rabbit—its neck snapped an hour ago—in the oven. A father stokes the fire and smokes a pipe. Cedar and tobacco. The daughter sets the table. The son cleans a gun. Out of the corner of her eye the photographer is always looking doorward. For trouble. She shoots a look over to her camera, dangling from a hook on the wall. This image maker. This thief. This lover. She thinks of the event that took place yesterday that nearly destroyed the son, and of the photos she took, and how she smuggled the film out as if she were smuggling humans to safety.

After dinner, the son, a teenager, begins to tell the story of the event. *We knew that the soldiers were using the real bullets; we knew that the tanks crushed the people. Freedom came from all of us in this square; all of us, teenagers who still went to school, like myself, the students, the teachers, the factory workers, the bus drivers, the mothers, widows, amputees, all of us!* The father embraces the son. The mother claps as if she is at a play and her cheeks fill with blood. *This is my son.* The sister does a dance in front of the fire, some kind of domestic and darling resistance. Then the front door blows open and soldiers with rifles clamor in and fast as a shutter clicking first the photographer's camera, and then her left cheekbone are smashed in by the butt of a rifle, changing her face forever.

2.

The man from the Tambov Gang drives the poet in a black BMW through the streets of his city speaking of its ghosts: Maksim Gorky. Pushkin's wife. Sculptors, pianists, painters, musicians, poets. The oldest drama house in the country. Then he asks her if she knows of Maria Spiridonova. The Russian revolutionary? she asks. Yes, he says, the woman who shot in the face a general responsible for brutally suppressing a peasant uprising. Who was dragged facedown on cobbled steps, stripped and raped and whipped, cigarettes stubbed out on her breasts. Who was exiled to Siberia. Who spent most of her adult life in a state of being beaten. The poet puts her hand to her throat and asks, What became of her? History, he says. She was executed. And his voice and the night bleed into each other until they are out of the city, arriving at a redbrick house surrounded by oak trees and flax fields. When they leave the car, before they enter the house, he tells her that the materials she requires will be delivered to her the following day: the doctored passport, the travel papers, the false identification verifications. He says, And when you find the location of the girl, my men will pick her up and take her to the train station at Vilnius. But *after* tonight. He smiles.

As they enter the building, it does not alarm the poet that they go straight down into the basement. In her life, there are many nights in basements, where ordinary people act out physical fantasies in homemade dungeons or playrooms or simply low-lit rooms away from the socius. But when they get to the belly of things, a great dark room with a concrete floor covered in places with giant oriental carpets, a towering wooden cross beam hanging from the ceiling, and one large black wooden table in the center covered with a white linen cloth and more instruments of whipping than even she has ever seen, she is surprised. For there is not one man waiting, but nearly a dozen men, all wearing brown or black Cossacks with roped belts. She freezes behind the man from the Tambov Gang. Has she been led into real or imagined danger? He turns around, takes in her fear, and gently touches her arm. Leads her ahead of him. She bites the inside of her cheek. What is this? she says, trying to sound in control rather than captured. He gently eases her down by the shoulders into a chair. Sit, my friend. Do not be alarmed. You are among friends. But we are not the same as you. We punish the skin for different reasons. Maria Spiridonova flashes up in her mind's eye. But she holds her face, her shoulders, still. Somehow. He continues. We are Khlysts. She feels the air in her lungs again. Khlysts. One of countless break-off religious sects that practices ecstatic ritual. Sexual orgies. Flagellation. Cleansing the soul through pain and sexual excess. She wrote a fucking poem about Khlysts. The poet quickly reexamines the room, looking for a woman. Each Khlyst cell, she dimly remembers, is led by a male and a female leader, the "Christ" and the "Mother of God." Where is the fucking woman? The poet tries to recover her position in this story. Reaching down her own throat to rescue herself, to become the American poet dominatrix, she asks in a husky voice, Where is the Mother of God? The man from the Tambov Gang smiles, then bows, then goes to his knees before her. *It's me*, she realizes. *I'm the woman.* He looks up at her. Remember what you promised, beautiful hard woman. We made this deal, you and I. He takes her hands in his. Suffering to cleanse suffering. They stare at each other. And then he speaks the name of a man, and one of the men steps forward, to be washed, anointed, and then tied to a cross and hung from the ceiling for her to beat clean.

3.
The Neva River flows from Lake Ladoga through St. Petersburg to the Gulf of Finland. It is the third largest river in Europe, after the Volga and the Danube. During midwinter, the river freezes. Grigori Rasputin drowned in the Neva in 1916; after assassins shot him several times and attempted to poison him, they beat him, wrapped him in a sheet, and dumped him into the freezing waters. Later his body was burned. Peter the Great died at the age of fifty-three after diving into the Neva River in winter to rescue drowning sailors. The icy waters are said to have exacerbated his bladder problems.

A young man found the body of the performance artist on the banks of the Neva thirty-three miles downstream from where she jumped, and pulled her up onto the shore with little effort. Though only sixteen, Afanasy already weighed two hundred pounds and stood six feet three in his socks. Afanasy sat on the bank and rubbed his head and rocked and puzzled over what to do; her body was bloated and stiff now, and he was not at all sure how to carry her home, like an oversize plank across his shoulders? When he arrived at the house, his mother came running out and thought for a moment that she was looking at the Christ, then she saw that it was her only son, and she shouted his name and shouted his name and shrieked, *What have you done? What have you done, my son?* Sobbing and throwing her hands into the sky. For Afanasy had been born without any wits, and her manboy of a son had already crushed a village girl when he found her lying facedown in the snow, raped and bleeding. Even though she believed her beautiful too-big son, that he had tried to save her and keep her shivering body warm until help came, no one believed it was not him who killed her, and the only reason he was not sent to Siberia was that his mother had given them their life's savings and begged with her very life to keep her dim-witted son with her. *What use is he to you?* And all the soldiers had laughed, perhaps the one who had raped the girl the hardest. But what if a second girl was discovered? And so mother and son built a fire at midnight and threw this unknown girl's body into the flames. For a moment she appeared to sit up, no doubt due to the frozen tendons in her legs heating up in the fire, but for the boy with the softened mind and the distraught mother it was a terrible omen. The boy had nightmares the rest of his life of a girl coming out of a fire to kill him, and the mother never forgave herself for letting this girl's name slip from existence. And the performance artist's body went from water through ice to fire, and then into ash, and as the morning came and the sky went white whatever she had been was covered with snow.

White Space

In the white, life moves in pieces. Little fragmentations and synchronicities and echo effects. The story you have of yourself is loosened and made random. There is something deeply comforting in this—to see your life again in glimpses and patterns that are free-flowing. Something beautiful happens when syntax and order, chronology and narrative sense give way. Part of me wants to stay here forever.

When the men come for me, I am in the barn painting. I am working on the painting of a girl with a house in her mouth. I am using images from memory. A house. And inside the house was a family. And inside the family was a girl. A girl who must have been me, and yet that girl is lost to me. In her place, I paint. I am this body of heat. These hands of fire. Like blood makes a body, I use blood and paint to make a girl.

I can hear something coming. And there is a faint, soft, sweet smell, like only a child's skin can smell. The white seems to breathe.

Then I see the girl. She is running toward me. Running with all her might. Her golden hair tendrils out wild behind her. The blue of her eyes like opals nearly shatters me. My legs feel weak. I take a step back, not sure if I can withstand her.

What it has meant to stay alive when my daughter did not. What it has meant to suffer a heartbeat after carrying the weight and form of her inside my body, wedged just beneath that fist-shaped muscle. The girl runs toward me with a fierce velocity. Closer and closer with speed and light and then she runs straight into me, wrapping her arms around me tightly, taking my very breath away.

When the men come I can hear them and smell them long before they reach the barn. There is a sound that is men. There is. At the door with guns there is nothing to do but what they say. I wait, but no harm comes. They tell me I am to go to America. They say a woman poet will take me. I look at my painting. My hands. I think about all the girls left to nothingness.

I look at the men. They smell of cologne and leather and hair cream. They look—they look like they are in a movie. How the men look in the widow's books about the history of film. Am I in a movie, then? They say that they will return the following morning to take me to a train station in Vilnius. This American poet they speak of will be there. This will begin my journey.

This is my death. This embrace. And I close my eyes and lower my head and wrap my body around her the way a mother fits a child, and I let the air leave my lungs thinking yes, like this, I will let go like this and it will make an ending.

But the girl's strength surpasses mine in a mythic burst. Any child is stronger than a mother, since the love we have for our children could kill us. She sends me an electrical jolt and grabs my hand and pulls me in a dead run farther into the white.

We run until I see a bonfire coming into focus. It is a good fire. I know this because the girl is laughing, and her laughter sings my bones. I begin to laugh too, until I am crying and laughing, and together we swing 'round in circles holding hands. *Ashes ashes we all fall down!*

That night, the widow reads to me from Emily Dickinson and Walt Whitman. She plays me music made by a man as black as night, even his name a song: Coltrane. She says this is the better story for my life, to go to this other country, to become an artist in the company of artists. She tells me to never forget where I came from, to carry the spirit of this place in my heart. Where do any of us come from? Is it a country? A mother? Or is it perhaps an image, a song, a story inside which we feel . . . named?

We laugh ourselves out, then sit quietly looking at each other, our breathing finding its rhythms again. Her smile—it is the end of me. I see what should happen next. I wait for the air to still, the fire's warmth to cradle us. I look her in the eye. I take the longest breath of my life. Did I kill you? She shakes her head so simply: no. Are you happy? She nods her head yes. May I stay with you?

And my girl stands up, takes my hand again, and walks me slowly and lovingly toward a window—a small yellow glow—a cluster of butterflies. I look back at her, and follow her gaze.

Leaving the widow—this woman who delivered me from ash to art—it is heavy in my chest. This childless woman who stood in the place of a mother, like a painted symbol in a new language. How she gave me a story of my own blood, read to me, played music, let me go inside all the books and photographs and paintings and music of her house, how we pulled the boards from dead buildings so that I could paint on them, how we lived so smally, quietly, together in the eye of history, with no one to know us, with no one who killed us, just our two bodies present inside loss.

The night before I leave I give her the painting of the girl with the house in her mouth. She hangs it in the very center of the largest room. We don't speak. Then she helps me burn every other painting I have ever made.

The small yellow shape pulses with life. Still thinking of butterflies, I place my hand on the glass of the window, and then she places her smaller hand upon mine, and the years of pain and loss barrel up from my belly until they thicken and choke my throat, until my mouth opens and the wail of mother comes, and still she keeps her hand on mine and I can feel her hair brushing against my arm, and I am certain I am dying, either I am dying from this grief I have held so long or I am dying from the joy of her, and when the sound begins to quiet and drift away and my throat opens back up to ordinary air, I hear her say, "Look, Mama, open your eyes," and I open my eyes and out the window is my writing. Words and words. Pages and pages of white, the roads and paths carved through in intricate hieroglyphics. This has been

Fire always looks like butterflies to me.

I don't know why some of us live while others die. It all seems to me an accident, someone digging in the dirt with a spade, someone else given a gun to shoot him in the head. One girl goes to school and becomes a doctor, another is raped and beaten and left to rot in the snow like a dog. One family escapes war and finds a new home, a new nation, the price of freedom to erase the homeland from their memories; another family blown to bits without the barest notice.

my life. It is not a black hole of grief. It is making art.

I will never again have a father, a mother, a brother. I will never again live in my home. My country is not in me except in the violence that has crossed my body. But the smell and feel of oak trees and flax fields, my feet in the river, the colors of this place in flowers and roots and leaves and berries that I have ground down and heated into pigment, the will to live so that I can paint . . .

Art, she is in me.

Motherlands

In a floating memory, the writer shuts off the light in her son's bedroom, the boy finally breathing the sleep of little boys before they are asked to do the unthinkable, step into the story of men. She thinks of boys sleeping everywhere, how beyond-language beautiful they are. She knows she is like other mothers in part, but not entirely. In her there is a fracture. The fracture is another child. A girl. His sister who never was. Her chest constricts. Her heart beats past rupture. She can't leave his room. Can't walk into the hallway away from him. Who can count how long she stands there.

The first day of kindergarten she cried. She walked him and his miniature backpack into the field of small bodies. She kissed him good-bye. His eyes filled with tears. The kindergarten teacher led him into the classroom, telling her, "It will be okay."

She walked to her car, got in, closed the door, and sat still for four hours. Waiting the wait of women who have carried death.

Atomization

Explosions in the distance.

The poet shoves her hands in her pockets. She waits in some kind of holding room at a small rural train station. The room is the color of dirty snow or ash. There is a large and scarred mirror on one wall, a long gray-green table in the middle of the room, two chairs, and a picture of the city from the fifties. Above her head, exposed pipes. There is also a tinted window, which the poet suddenly realizes is probably surveillance glass; she wonders what interrogations happened here over the course of history. She looks at the cement floor for stains, traces of human.

The girl has a man on each arm. The one on her left has a cigarette eternally dangling between his lips. The man on her right is heavy beside her. She wonders if her shoulder, arm, are bruised from the weight of him.

The poet's studious gaze moves from the floor to the green metal door of the room; the doorknob rattles and then the door opens and there are two men and a girl. The poet sucks in a breath sharply. My god. The girl is so beautiful it feels violent. Like god appearing to an atheist.

Gunfire muffled in the distance.

The girl is led to a chair, told to sit. She looks at the floor. Then slowly, from the floor up, she looks at this American woman standing in the room. In her black leather jacket with her short hair and slim frame, she looks like . . . Hollywood from the books.

One of the men—the heavy one—says something to the other in Russian. The lighter of the two looks at him for a long minute, then at the girl, then at the poet, then leaves the room. The poet hears him lock the door. Her neck hair bristles. She takes her hands out of her pockets. She looks at the mass of man in front of her. He pulls a wad of documents from inside his coat, puts them on the table. The poet studies what must be their paperwork. Then the man asks her, "Do you have the rest of the money?" The poet stares at him, her mind seizing around reality.

The girl's toes curl up inside her shoes and she grips the underside of the chair.

An explosion rattles the walls, some distance and yet near.

The poet looks at the papers on the table and starts to narrate her position, but in the middle of her carefully crafted sentences a fist finds her face and she is sent hard to the floor. She tastes metal and her ears buzz. Then she is lifted from the floor like a puppet and punched in the gut. Then the door opens and the second man comes in and in his hands are thick braided ropes. While the lighter man moves toward her with the ropes, the heavy man hits her again twice in the face. Her eyes swim. Then he pulls out his gun and instructs her to strip if she wants to live. The poet doesn't move and the man points the gun at the girl. The poet removes her clothes to save the girl. The poet closes her eyes and looks inward. When she opens her eyes she keeps her gaze locked on the eyes of her tormentor. Dead stare. Then they tie her wrists to two lengths of rope and bind her ankles together; the lengths of rope are then looped up and around metal pipes near the ceiling, so that her arms are extended on either side, her feet bound but still on the ground.

The girl opens her mouth and yells *Ne!* and is then sent across the room in a single blow, her head shattering the mirror.

The smaller man is instructed to leave. The man turned beast takes off his belt. He begins without ceremony to whip the poet. Welts rise red and swollen on her breasts, her torso, her belly and abdomen. She does not make a sound. Instead she bites the inside of her cheeks until blood fills her mouth.

When the girl comes to, she is flat on the cement floor. She thinks she sees what people call Christ being beaten in front of her. Velázquez. Then she remembers what is happening. Pieces of glass surround her head. She picks one up. Because she is small and quiet like animals are and no threat to the action—for what is a girl—neither the poet nor the man beating the poet hear her take off all of her clothes, so that when the man unzips his pants and moves toward the poet yelling obscenities in Russian, the girl's voice surprises him. *Here*, she says, and lies down on the table, her sex hairless and her breasts barely rising, her spread legs unimaginably open.

Language leaves the poet at the image of the girl's body.

The man laughs in a guttural slobber and lurches toward the body of the girl and throws himself on the slight of her. The poet starts yelling American obscenities in violent bursts, trying to make words kill things. The girl makes her eyes dead. And as the man pierces into her she stabs him in the side of the throat with the glass. Again. Again.

The man places the beef of his hand on the girl's face trying to smother the life from her, then dies on top of her, his blood on her face and breasts. Stillness.

The girl stands on a chair and unties the poet. The poet's arms drop around the shoulders of the girl, and for a moment the two look as if they are in an embrace. The poet lifts the girl's face up and looks into her eyes. The poet opens her mouth. But no words come. Silence.

The poet and the girl re-dress, collect themselves.

When the door begins to rattle, the poet picks up a chair and stands ready to smash in the skull of whoever enters, and the girl raises her arm with glass in her hand, but as the door opens whoever it is turns to sound as an entire wall explodes around them.

Artillery fire. Or a stray missile. Or a bomb. Avisual. Reverse origin.

The poet and the girl run from the room through the blast hole, fire around their forms.

How a story can change in the violence of an instant. How content is a glimpse of something.

And in the end a train carries them. And a plane lifts them into the sky. On the plane the poet tells the girl the story of how she came to find her, and why. The girl listens, not catching all of what this woman is saying to her, since her English is still forming. But individual words and lines and images go into her. And the quivering in the poet's hands when she lifts the little airplane drink up to her face again and again. And the tiny lines near her eyes that have written themselves this day. And the marks on the poet's body that the girl knows hide violence like a skin song beneath her clothes. And the girl carries something with her as small as a seed.

Part Four

Making Art

The first year I lived with the American artists is a collage.

This is a house.

These are the rooms.

This one, your room.

A room of your own.

We are giving it to you.

Because we can.

This is the table of the artists, where we eat and speak and act out relations.

This is the school, the American Interdisciplinary Art School.

Isn't it something?

This is the in-home entertainment system with Sensurround sound and these are the Mac computers and this is a cell phone with a computer and this is software to make films in the sanctity of one's own home.

Can you believe it?

This is what's bad: The Nixon administration. The Reagan

administration. The Bush administrations. War. Poverty. Injustice. Christians. Oil. Racists. Global warming. Homophobia. Corporations. The plight of third world nations.

This is money.

This is how we shop online.

This is Organic.

This is a haircut, makeup, jewelry, scented soaps. This is how to be a girl in this country. Pink.

I am upstairs in the painting room they created for me, in a house surrounded by firs, ferns, alders. I am the only one home. I lick the skin of my arm. Salt. Then I hear the UPS truck grumbling its way toward the house. I know it will stop here; I can see when it arrives from this wide upstairs room where I paint. It comes once a month. For years. Once a month a delivery of canvas, paper, paint, brushes, linseed oil, turpentine, art books. For me.

The deliveries come from a man who has become the exiled American painter in my mind's eye. I have learned about him through their stories of him, how he rose to fame as an abstract painter, how he used women as if they were paint, how he shot his wife the writer. And I have read about him through my own research on the Internet, through all the media this country so lavishly spills all over everything.

It seems important to them that he is a kind of villain in their stories. This seems American.

There is something I have never told them. For seven years now, deep inside the delivery packaging, this man—the American painter—hides little notes, and I find them as I use the materials. *Sable brushes are preferable to any other—don't waste your time with the small ones. Detail work is for Dutch dead men. Use the light from the window in the room they've created for you—never artificial light. Never. Take ten steps back from your work every hour or you will lose sight of it. Don't think. Don't know. Just paint. If you must paint with your hands, use these—latex gloves. Oil paint can kill you, for fuck's sake.* The notes are rolled around tubes of paint or brushes, slid between pages in books, buried inside rolls of paper or written in pencil on canvas. These secret hieroglyphics from the man who shot his wife.

All I ever wanted was canvas. Even when the environment was dire.

The UPS truck is pulling up the gravel drive, through the alder trees. I close my eyes and breathe.

The second year I lived here is a mural with the images of three women on it in different states. The first woman is the writer. I saw her one morning emerging from the shower, dripping with water. A woman who suffered great loss and did not die. Baptismal.

The second image of a woman is the poet's body before I untied her in the room of her torture, her arms outspread, her naked body carrying the trace of violence as if her wounds had been painted. Velázquez.

The third image of a woman is a girl—for there is no girl we are not always already making into a woman from the moment she is born—making a city in the dirt next to the boot of a man.

It could be rage or love in his feet. The girl could be me or any other girl.

The third year I lived here is a double portrait, like a deformed reflection.

The left side is a girl with a wolf's paw in place of a hand. She stands naked in a pool of her own blood, her head lifted upward as she laughs a whole sky filled with snow geese and song. The right side is the writer, her journal resting in her hands, the words filling the space so that her face, her hair, her mouth, her eyes are made of language. A mother and a girl who are separate but joined.

The fourth year is a painting at the bottom of the stairs, in the living room opposite the wall that wears the famous photo of me as a child. How strange to look at one of my paintings next to this photograph of . . . is it of me? How?

My painting is different from the photo. In the photo, they say over and over again that the girl is a "victim of violence." But in my painting, a young woman comes out of fire with a vengeance in her stare. Her stone blue eyes finding you.

The fifth and sixth years are animal: wolves turning into girls, girls turning into fire.

The seventh year is now. The painting I am making now.

To make a small pool of blood to use with paint, place a bowl between your legs, not an artificially scented wad of cotton. You must move outside what you have been told.

I am painting the spread legs of a grown woman, the mouth of her opening up to the viewer, her breasts a terrain just before her face in the distant background.

With my hands.

On a six-feet-by-six-feet canvas.

In this room in a house they have given to me.

Inside her cleft will be hands.

Her hair will be woven with wolves.

The UPS truck is nearly at the house, and I am the only one here just now, so I will need to go to the door and sign for the delivery. I clean my hands with wipes, leaving the act of painting and moving into the act of looking.

I think of the canvas like a body. It is alive. It is a body and I am a body and my inner rhythms tell me how to move with this other body.

I have read about the history of painting.

There are things in my head that no one has taught me, that I have not read or seen or heard anywhere else. They come out from my hands.

For the fleshy inside of her thighs, then, I will use blood and indigo.

I turn and leave the room, making my way down the stairs of this house. The UPS truck's little horn blows three times. My feet on each stair step look cartoonlike to me—little Nike symbols making their marks.

Are there more brands of shoes in America than there are children in the world?

Seven years I have lived with this small group of American artists. I know all their stories. The playwright's story is the drama of a brother and sister; a family plot. The poet's story is a relentless body. The filmmaker's story is flex and light and speed: action and male. The writer's journal crosses the terrain of loss and love like a great white tundra.

The painter shot his wife and the photographer shot me, to make art.

I think art is a place where all our stories collect.

They mean to keep me safe, to give me a story that will hold me. There are many kinds of love, but there is never a love, or a life, without pain.

I mean to paint my way home. I am ready.

The End. One.

You must consider filmmaking. It is the dominant mode of artistic production in our time. You know more about filmmaking than most of what you were taught in school. You are the camera's eye. You are in control of everything we see. Hear. How things are framed. What the shot-reverse-shot relationships are, what every cut is, you are shooting. You are, after all, *American.* Eternal superpower, the camera's eye.

For the opening, you decide to move in slow motion and black-and-white. An excruciatingly beautiful girl gone to woman, walking. A girl who has toppled over into woman, her lips already in a pout between yes and no, her torso and ass breaking faith. Moving down a tree-lined city sidewalk. Fall. Her coat pulled up to the flush of her cheeks. Her hands stuffed down into pockets. Her hair making art in the wind.

Her eyes . . .

Her eyes.

Think of actresses who could fill the screen with them.

It is a remarkable passage, a symphony of aesthetics, when a girl stops walking like a girl and begins to walk like a woman.

I'm not sure anyone has ever captured that before. Perhaps we are afraid to name it, that coming of age, that passage. We've one great story, I suppose: *Lolita*. Several painters come to mind. Perhaps a few photographers. And of course film stars. In any case, none of it, nothing in the history of art, is quite right for this particular moment, is it? For this simple reason: she is not the object of desire now in the ways we are used to, is she? I mean, from the point of view of the American male artist she is, and from the point of view of the photographer, and maybe all the artists, but from the point of view we're inhabiting she's new. A man desires her more than he can stand, to be sure, and everyone who peoples her life just now desires her in one way or another, but that is not what is propelling the action or creating this plot, is what I'm saying.

It is her and you.

This has not been narrated in a previous scene, and yet, you know that blood is what's driving her.

Blood driving her down the tree-lined sidewalk.

Blood driving her to the door of the warehouse building where the artist's studio sits wombed among other artists' spaces.

Blood driving her sexualized body.

You wish I would stop speaking of all this blood, but I'm afraid it's the point.

Stop wishing it wasn't.

Just once, the story will keep its allegiance to the body of a single woman.

Not the object of her body, but her experience of her body.

With all of history deeply up and in her.

So then. You have kept the entire scene of her walking to the door of the building in black and white. As she approaches the door to the warehouse, you give color. You give the door and her lips Alizarin crimson. And as she enters the throat of the building, more things go to color, but you filter it with a kind of midnight blue bruise tone.

You can do that kind of thing.

You can manipulate everything.

You can make meaning no matter what the reality.

American.

As she enters the cargo elevator, floor by floor, you return from slow motion to regular time.

By the time she reaches his floor, lurchingly, the speed of things is how we think we experience it in reality (forgetting everything we know).

You know, you've so many choices here. A letch of a middle-aged man, about to meet the image of his dreams. A familiar story.

But that's not this story, is it?

His desire has not driven, well, anything. It's downright impotent.

It is her desire that has begun to set the entire building on fire.

It is her action.

It is her subjectivity that is taking its fullest form—and she is not doing what we'd hoped or wanted.

She has come there in a premeditated way from the belly of history itself.

She has come to make an image take form, to complete an image of a self.

She placed herself between violence and desire.

She has come from an atomized family.

From the slobbering violence of men.

From the lost youth of a girl.

From the foreign hopes born between women.

His door is ajar. He is of course there, drinking, not painting. He is thinking of painting, but the only thing he wants to paint is the girl from the photo. And so he goes to the studio every day and drinks himself into oblivion and either sleeps in his own excess or stumble-fucks his way back home. I don't know how these people stay alive, but they do. They do. And then they don't.

How you frame it is all in her hands.

She takes her right hand out of her coat pocket and you move to slow motion again. Her hand then takes up the entire shot, larger than life. Her hand (with blood-red traces) pushes the door open as if she is moving gender itself.

He turns and looks at her, but the camera's point of view is hers, not his, and so he looks small and puzzled, like a circus midget, at first. Then he looks like a tiny symbol of a man whose prayers have been answered, and he lowers his head, and no I am not kidding, he cries. Huge heaves like a kid. He cries and cries.

You will think there are pages missing, whole scenes.

But there are no pages or scenes missing.

This is the room of art.

Your life rules do not apply here.

Hold still.

I have related this earlier, but I will remind you: the first thing he says, the first words out of his mouth are, I have been painting you.

There is no conversation about this.

There is nothing that . . . confuses her or hoodwinks her or overpowers her.

She simply removes her clothes—and how you film this is mostly through color and odd angled blur, a little abstract and almost underwater looking—until she is nude there before him, except that again it is not his point of view, so it is not really *before him,* and to the audience it looks like some mythic woman god taking up nearly the entire frame except for the almost-cowering man in the lower-right-hand corner.

A miniature man of a man. Twitchy and nervous and simian.

Her body is enormous and milk-blue-aqua.

It almost glows.

You fill the screen with her out-of-focus back and ass and oceans of blond hair. And you take a further risk: you let the camera linger there, with the little monkey of a man frantically painting in the small right-lower corner, for an enormously long time.

It isn't very dramatic how they come to each other. It's actually rather simple: His erratic monkey-man gestures finally overtake him and he lunges at her and she absorbs him, like energy disappearing into its opposite.

She laughs, but the sound is loving, not mocking.

For four days, they wrestle-fuck—what is making love—what has it ever been—what is it in this moment—violent "making"—on the floor in the paint and the sweat and the secretions of a male body and a female body. They eat and drink minimally, mostly alcohol and water and pretzels and oranges.

A word about mouths and hands.

You will have to work hard to figure out a way to do credit to this on film. Because the fact is, their devouring mouths and their uncontrollable hands are much more important than their genitals. This has never been filmed before, nor captured in writing, but it is the truth beneath the lie of what usually passes for the "sex scene," and all I am doing is naming it.

This may not be true for everyone, but it is true for them: that their mouths and their hands are the center. The absolute fulcrum from which all energy emerges. And every other organ or opening is simply an extension or metaphor.

It goes without saying that they both bleed, numerous times.

Biting, scratching, tearing, cutting.

It goes without saying that they paint together with blood.

Four days.

A bloody, messy lovemaking.

That's it. That's the scene.

The End. Two.

When the girl was walking toward the door of the artist's warehouse, there was a voyeur.

The photographer.

As random as any image of our lives, she happened to have returned to the States then. She happened to be walking down the street going in the other direction. She was not, in fact, thinking of the American male painter, even as she knew his studio was brushing her right shoulder. Her life path took her past the studio plenty of times, and this time she was thinking of more important things.

But that day she saw the face of a girl-turned-to-woman that made her gasp. The fall air pulled into her lungs, then shot out again.

The prizewinning face, the face that changed her life forever.

Older, yes, much, but still.

Her face burned as it was into her retina, her skull, her heart.

And she is fully aware of what has transpired in the plot of all of their lives. The photographer knows the story. They told her in e-mails and faxes and phone calls. She had never let it enter her mind. At least not fully. She couldn't. Too much. The image incarnate. Too much.

In fact, though they are not aware of it, she has severed her relationship with this company. She cannot bear the weight of them, and her new life has somehow untethered itself from everything she was connected to before. She hasn't the heart to tell them; her plan is simply to live without them.

The only one of them she wants to see, was on her way to see, is the writer.

They say she has recovered.

They say she is alive with writing.

They say the girl's story—and her alive son—and the drive of her husband—brought life back to her. That they pieced her back together from a dead place. Strange made-up family.

She didn't let it into her and she didn't let it be true and she didn't think. She said to herself, Don't think. Too much.

And so, as she walks briskly to see the writer, whom in truth she wants to devour with a kiss though she is incapable of doing so, she sees the girl from the photo. Her photo. The girl who was lost after the photo.

She sees her enter the warehouse building of the American male painter.

She stands there dully for several minutes.

Still shot.

And then she walks back to her car and sits in it for four days, eating PowerBars, squatting by the sidewalk to pee when no one is looking, walking to a corner café to shit or eat or drink more, unable to leave until she witnessed the girl again.

But the girl does not reappear. She thinks perhaps she missed her in one of her sprints to the café, but somehow she also thinks she did not, that she is inside, with him, that this is how history moves, a man and a woman, violence and desire, time and the moon and nations in fragments and nonsensical bursts.

Her hair looks like hell.

Her pussy and her armpits itch.

How long will she wait for the image of the girl?

When the photographer finally takes the elevator up and opens the door to the loft and walks up the stairs to where she can smell the scent of human, what she sees first is the body of the girl covered in red, which she takes to be blood, splayed out ass-side up on a futon. Then she sees the artist leaning on the ledge of the loft wall, then she sees the gun—a gun—on the floor. She sees the gun and all she can think is, This is the gun. The son of a bitch has kept the gun, all these years, and now his true colors are all over the fucking place—he's shot another one. He's shot another woman. Since he is not moving—he looks as if he's in some kind of trance, or he's so drunk he can't stay upright—she moves calmly toward the gun on the floor and picks it up and aims it at him.

"What have you done. What the fuck have you done."

To which he responds by opening his mouth, closing his eyes, and raising his hands palm-side up. He looks like a middle-aged Jesus, bloated and puffy with drink.

She makes a bad assumption because of . . . well, everything.

Her past, her present, everything they are and have been and everything she wishes she could have been and everything she has become. She assumes the girl is dead, since she isn't moving.

Then, with the calm of a woman who knows what's what, she aims very simply and without drama and shoots him in the chest.

He topples over the loft wall to whatever.

And here is a detail you probably wish I would leave out:

The photographer has her camera with her. She turns and photographs the body of the seemingly dead girl.

The book of photography that will come from this image will be filled with young women in the throes of desire or danger, and it will be titled *She Placed Herself Between Violence and Desire*, and it will lead to a great deal of money and a documentary film and quite a bit of fame.

The body of the male artist she leaves broken and bleeding on the ground floor of the loft. She doesn't look. She doesn't look.

The End. Three.

What is the measure of loss?

It is in the hands, the girl-gone-to-woman thinks. It may be the only thing she knows. It is not the heart. It has never been the heart. It is astonishing how much myth has been devoted to that fist-size muscle, that blood pump.

After they have painted several blood paintings and several not-blood paintings, after they have fucked each other every way possible without once thinking of love, either of them, after they have come and pissed and shat and sweated and screamed and scratched and cut and bitten and everything else, they are reduced finally again to their animal selves.

In a quiet moment of breathing and drinking wine and staring into space, she asks him if he still has the gun.

He looks at her.

But he does not say, What gun? It is the gun from the story.

Of course he still has the gun.

She asks if he will show it to her.

His hand slips under the futon where he keeps it. Of course he shows it to her.

She fingers it. She turns it and turns it between her strangely bloodied hands. Her hands that have every possible trace of human on them.

He is not thinking, This woman is about to shoot me.

She is not thinking, I am going to shoot this man.

But neither are they not thinking those things, if by thinking we mean the mind brought to the very cusp of action. Even mindless action.

So when she points the gun at him, and he doesn't move, and he closes his eyes, and he smiles very faintly, and when she pulls the trigger, without any kind of emotion in her at all, a person might wonder what it is that she *does* think and feel.

What she thinks and feels is this: This is a world of men. They come into your country, they invade your home, they kill your family. They turn your body into the battlefield—the territory of all violence—all power—all life and death. And we take it. We do. We keep taking it. We have lost track of the reasons we do not slaughter the world of men, but we do not. Yes, there are good men. She sees the face of her father. She sees how the filmmaker loves the writer. She sees the yet-unwritten life of the writer's son. She sees her . . . brother. Beautiful smear. But it is the world of men that creates pure destruction. And this is a truth we cannot bear: Since we bear them into the world, we cannot kill them. Cannot be done with them. Cannot exile them into oblivion.

We simply keep going, letting them enter us and seed us, unable to stop loving the meat and drive of them, for without men, would the world even spin in its orbit? The action of a man—without it, would there simply be a hollowed-out black hole? Empty space?

She doesn't know.

She says a prayer for the soul of this man, just as she said prayers for her dead father, her dead brother, lovingly. As lovingly as possible.

She aims the gun at him.

Then she pulls the trigger.

Blood shoots everywhere between them.

His face is not shocked or filled with hate or rage.

He looks peaceful.

He looks done.

Neighbors call the authorities. A Homeland Security SWAT team arrives, and the girl is arrested. A week and a half later, she is deported.

The poet will be arrested for illegal aid to an illegal alien. An Interpol search will be conducted to find the performance artist. The poet will write a book of poems from her time in jail. It will solidify her career as a political poet. She will win numerous prizes, in America and abroad.

The writer will be told what happened. She will go into her bedroom and close the door, very calmly. The filmmaker will nearly lose his mind with worry, but in only two days she will come back out of the bedroom. She will not go down. She will spend the rest of her life communicating with this young Eastern European artist. The art each makes will inform the other's. The writer's stories, the young woman's paintings, between them everything. It will keep both of them making art until each of their deaths.

The girl will live on, in a country emerging on the world stage. Someday the economics of her country will count for something, or they will join up with another country and matter. Someday this girl's paintings will meet an audience, whether over the Internet, or by cosmic accident, or through back channels and counterculture trades, through thievery or trade or black-market wishes. But they will find their way into the world, her paintings.

Superpowers will topple and reorganize.

China and India will become something we never imagined.

Russia will make new allegiances. Siberia, unfreezing, will become a land grab.

France will take on a militant tone, leaving its beautiful cultural tower to chase power after all these years.

Canada and Russia and Greenland will stake new claims in once-frozen waters.

Africa will become an out-of-reach commodity instead of the expendable refuse heap we've treated her as.

Germany will forgive itself so much that it returns to arms.

And the Middle East, well, I think we can all see what we've made there. What a hand we've had in the making of our own demise. How masterful.

And the world will continue to be melted by a sun we've crossed terribly with our progress.

Nations will shift like stones in the hands of a girl making a city in the dirt.

And men and women . . . either they will finally see each other and do what must be done to evolve, or they will not.

The filmmaker and the writer will invent a kind of love from making art together and loving a son.

The End. Four.

The painter takes one last look at her asleep on the futon and thinks: *Enough.*

He reaches under the futon, where he has always kept the gun. It fits into his hand like an identity. It's nothing, really, his magnificent and glorious death drive, up against the stories the girl told him about what happened to her. What is a man? he thinks. Wishing he was the story. This girl. This astonishing, gendered thing. What she has endured.

The sleeper.

He places the gun inside his mouth.

He shoots, the blood spray making its beauty behind him. If only someone were there to recognize this kind of beauty, to admit it. If only someone were there to capture it.

The End. Five.

The hospital curtain shivers, almost imperceptibly. The rise and fall of the writer's breathing. The image of a heart monitor, the audio silenced.

Two women alone in a room. The lives that might have been.

And the photographer's hand, as hushed as whisper, or was it love, resting a Polaroid of the writer upon her unconscious body.

Fatherlands

The widow's husband hid the last photo he'd ever taken of her, and smuggled it into the prison camp with him. What had been his life's passion, photography, was now over, his equipment smashed in heaps of glass and black plastic, even his eyeglasses smashed in front of him under the heel of a boot. Twenty-eight years, they said. His sentence.

The sentence became his body. The photograph of his wife against his iliac crest.

It took only five years for the widow's husband's mind to wander in that prison camp, in ways that remind him of DNA drifting, or the disintegration of the stars.

After that, he began to have nightmares: a bloody torso inching its way along the frozen ground, a leg without a body being pulled by a dead horse. He wakes in the night as if waking were sleeping and sleeping, labor. A few days ago, he thinks, he may have met a man from a town he perhaps knew in his previous life. The man had stolen wood and was awaiting sentencing.

Two days ago they had taken the man away. Yesterday he had returned. They had cut off one of his legs as punishment. The man's leg looked like an enormous stick of bread, he remembered thinking. They brought it back with them and threw it out where it could be seen from the barracks. Fresh corpses were piled onto sleighs daily, and prisoners harnessed like horses would pull them with ropes, drag them several hundred meters from the barracks and pile them up as if for a bonfire. But never the leg. It was left to rot there in front of them, but not, freezing instead, not decomposing as an ordinary human leg might. It is strange what moves us and what does not.

My wife is not here.

And then his thoughts would fragment and tumble again.

Buttercups.

Entrails.

A boot.

A common treatment for frostbite was to hang a body, barely living, from the ceiling. One girl with sores all over her was hung by the armpits. One man, so starved and shrunken as to appear to be a boy, was hung by his feet.

Men would come and go in his barracks, either in his mind's eye or in real time.

One was a writer.

With this man, he found bitter shared joy. He without a camera and he without a way to record his thoughts on paper. Art and ideas between them.

If he could produce a picture of their world, it would show hundreds of people curled fetal in their bunks like strange snails because scurvy had infected their joints. The white nights blew beyond thought. People reached the point where they had no sex, just the vague skeletal cage of a bodylike thing, mouths sunken in from lost teeth and disease, eyes glassy in their hollowed-out holes. He and the writer spoke many times of this imagined image. The writer absorbed it as a narrative.

One day the writer was taken away, and he did not see him again. His own strength faltered differently now. As with the loss of a lover or wife. He thought he saw him several times, far in the distance, in the night, the moon shining over a frozen forever delirium of cold. He thought he could see the writer framed by sky and the white of the snow, a skeletal figure, a stick man, harnessed like a horse, dragging the leg, with . . . was it buttercups? Falling from the sky? All the images of his life blurring now into one.

How the body goes on living sometimes.

Did he forget himself?

The face of his wife. No, newspaper crackled and blowing across the frozen prison yard.

He finds himself standing exposed, as if shitting in a field in the hours of a long day's labor, his genitals slowly sucking back into the cavities of his body, shrinking, retreating back. He is squatting, vulgar. He has no idea how long he has been this way. In sight the others are gathering wood, thistles, cones from the edge of a forest under the watch of armed guards. A soldier with a rifle, with a cigarette for a mouth. The rifle is perhaps less than five feet from his own dumb skull. He thinks he sees a flash of red. A woman leaning in to kiss the face of a lascivious soldier; no. A German shepherd dog's tongue pink against dirty snow, licking a palm. A man's penis pissing against dirty snow.

He dresses again. He looks out across white and on the white, peopled spots of black and gray and the hint of flesh. Faces? Holes for eyes and mouths. Is it a crowd? Fellow prisoners? Or just shapes? Trees?

He opens his mouth like it's a shutter.

I was an artist.

I existed.

I made art.

The guard cocks a trigger in a perfectly synchronous motion. The sound prompts the man to join the sticklike figures nearly cracking from their own actions. He is now part of the still life: prisoners gathering wood.

He remembers washing a man's back. The rag following the moles of his back as if they made some strange constellation, his own hand magnified to him, more than human, the man's flesh taking the hand's motions as a gentle whisper, like a woman's gesture, a woman washing a body, he remembers the skin reddening where he rubbed. The giving over to love, isn't it? The tiniest of gestures exploding like small compassionate bombs between them? Did he look upon the back of the man with longing? Where were the definitions of words going in this place? The black curls of the back of the man's head, so black, so coarse, so like a forest that he wanted to rest his face there, calmly and without intention, as natural as putting a head to a pillow in bed at night with his wife.

And cupping his own elbows in the alone. Oh, to let go to death.

In his tenth year, he is scratching his name into a wooden plank in the wall—or thinks he is; the word he actually is scratching is *Father*—when somewhere nearby an elderly man, emaciated but for his oddly round and melon-hard belly, laughs out loud, a thunderous laugh, almost hideous. He does his best to ignore the monstrous laughing man, focusing instead on a single letter of his work. Finally he turns to the cackling jackal of a man and tells him to go fuck himself. Can't the man see he is busy?

My dearest friend, the man says, I beg of you, forgive my intrusion. As it happens, I was just thinking that all my life has been given over to a pure insanity. You will wonder what I mean. In my case, it was science. Science! I have, as I say, given my life over to it, if you can believe the absurdity of that, the pursuit of that brand of knowledge in which the proven outscores the given. And at the age of seventy—at least I think that is the age, who knows in this place—it happened into my mind that the waste has not been these years in Siberia, but rather the years I spent toiling away in my lab, making "meanings" of things, working for the state believing with all my heart that physics was beyond anything, beyond patriotism or God, beyond the heart, the head, the concerns of the body, beyond any thought or drive. I am giving my life to the magnificent order of the universe, I thought, freely and with zeal! And when I saw you sitting there, friend, it reminded me of all my righteous-mindedness and idiotic sacrifice to the pinpoint world of microscopes and mathematics. He laughed again. Do you see?

In the time that he knew the old man, it seemed to him that there was not a single moment in which he was not talking. Narrating his knowledge, even in the face of its destruction and uselessness. It was as if an entire human history were pouring forth from his mouth. He believed himself to be dying, in fact, a cancer, yes, he was certain, his great and authentic big-headed knowledge of science assured him like second sight, even without his instruments, that his body was indeed being invaded, bombed, taken over, so to speak. Whether the old man was right, he hadn't a clue. He only knew that he wished the old man would go on speaking forever, since he had discovered that his primary fear was that he was losing his aesthetic awareness, his ability to see pictures and chart the world image by image—he was afraid he was no longer a photographer.

Once he had dreamed of winning a prize, *the* prize. But that might have been a man he read about. He couldn't be sure.

Buttercups and the lips of his wife.

Did he have a wife?

The day of their liberation came suddenly and without fanfare.

After the prisoners had forgotten their own names, officers began shooting prisoners at random, even as other officials were fleeing in jeeps, even as the camp was being overrun by liberation troops, their quarters burned to the ground, their leader handcuffed and scorned and whisked away for war crimes or picked up off the ground after suicides, still, the soldiers were shooting prisoners as best they could, and the old man *still* went on narrating everything he could remember about history, as he headed for a truck that would take him to safety, the photographer's hand held out to him with a few fingers still tingling with life, the old man babbling away and becoming nonsensical, storming from the mouth with the last vestiges of history, saying something, what was it, something about Galileo, and wasn't that extraordinary, that Galileo looked into a night sky and reversed an entire epoch, wasn't it something? And who among us would ever raise their head to a night sky like that again, he was saying, when they shot him. And an intense memory seized him in that moment of danger—he *was* a photographer! He knew what the shot would be!—the old man's head rocked back with the bullet shot and his mouth too red and agape, almost like he was laughing, toward a dead heaven, toward a godless sky, into the white.

And then the ping at his lower vertebrae, and then nothing.

Acknowledgments

My astonished gratitude to my agent and dear soul sister Rayhané Sanders and to the brilliant editor Calvert Morgan, without whom this book would not have made the leap into the hands of readers. Thank you for finding me and throwing a line into the waves.

Endless thanks to Chelsea Cain, Suzy Vitello, Monica Drake, Mary Wysong-Haeri, and Chuck Palahniuk for their support and help with this book. For years.

Of course my whole heart to Andy Mingo, who helped me transform what began as an epic poem whisper thing into an actual sort of novel. Deep in the woods of Oregon.

Thanks to Liz Fischer Greenhill, who read an early copy of the novel and helped keep me from fear with her heart-shimmer.

Gratitude to Raphael Dagold, who let me use and torque one of his astonishing poems in this story, and to Menas in Lithuania, whose paintings drove me down to the depths and back up.

I am in debt to the poets, novelists, painters, musicians, and filmmakers whose phrases are woven throughout this novel, including but not limited to H. D., Carolyn Forché, Walt Whitman, Marguerite Duras, Francis Bacon, Emily Dickinson, Virginia Woolf, Alain Resnais, and Doris Lessing.

And to my sister Brigid, who gave me literature, life.

And to Lily. Whose death rose writing in my hands.